FAMILY JEWELS

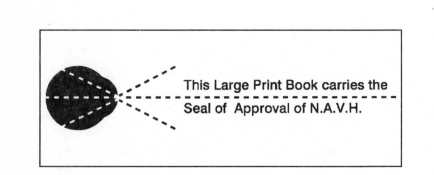

This Large Print Book carries the
Seal of Approval of N.A.V.H.

Copyright © 2016 by Stuart Woods.
A Stone Barrington Novel.
Thorndike Press, a part of Gale, Cengage Learning.

Thorndike Press® Large Print Basic.
The text of this Large Print edition is unabridged.
Other aspects of the book may vary from the original edition.
Set in 16 pt. Plantin.

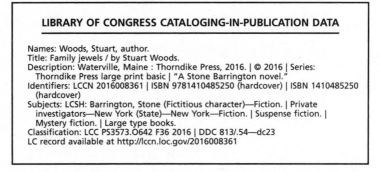

LIBRARY OF CONGRESS CATALOGING-IN-PUBLICATION DATA

Names: Woods, Stuart, author.
Title: Family jewels / by Stuart Woods.
Description: Waterville, Maine : Thorndike Press, 2016. | © 2016 | Series:
    Thorndike Press large print basic | "A Stone Barrington novel."
Identifiers: LCCN 2016008361 | ISBN 9781410485250 (hardcover) | ISBN 1410485250
    (hardcover)
Subjects: LCSH: Barrington, Stone (Fictitious character)—Fiction. | Private
    investigators—New York (State)—New York—Fiction. | Suspense fiction. |
    Mystery fiction. | Large type books.
Classification: LCC PS3573.O642 F36 2016 | DDC 813/.54—dc23
LC record available at http://lccn.loc.gov/2016008361

Published in 2016 by arrangement with G. P. Putnam's Sons, an imprint
of Penguin Publishing Group, a division of Penguin Random House LLC

Printed in the United States of America
1 2 3 4 5 6 7 20 19 18 17 16

FAMILY JEWELS

STUART WOODS

THORNDIKE PRESS
A part of Gale, Cengage Learning

GALE
CENGAGE Learning®

Farmington Hills, Mich • San Francisco • New York • Waterville, Maine
Meriden, Conn • Mason, Ohio • Chicago

This book is for Earl and Deborah Potter.

1

Stone Barrington fell into his chair at his desk. He had flown his airplane across the Atlantic from England the day before, and however much sleep he had had that night had not been enough. Joan Robertson, his secretary, came into his office bearing a mug of steaming coffee.

"Welcome back," she said. "You look terrible."

"Thanks for confirming that for me. It's jet lag."

"I thought you didn't get that, if you flew your own airplane."

"A myth, apparently." He tasted the coffee and burned his tongue. He made a face. "Do you have to make it this hot?"

"That is the temperature that the coffeepot operates at, and you've never complained about it before. Let it sit there for a minute or two and it'll cool down. Your first patient of the day is waiting to see you."

"Patient? What am I, a dentist?"

"More of a psychiatrist, I guess. Somehow, I think of them all as patients."

"I don't have any appointments this morning."

"This one is a walk-in."

"Do we take walk-ins here? I don't remember doing that."

"Sure we do. Some of your most interesting patients have been walk-ins. And anyway, you look as though you could use something to take your mind off the hangover."

"It's not a hangover, it's jet lag. I don't drink when I fly."

"Take your mind off the jet lag, then."

"Oh, all right, send him in."

"Sexist! You assume it's a man."

"All right, send *her* in."

"Now you're assuming it's a woman."

"I'm running out of choices — humor me."

"Right." Joan walked out of the office, and he heard her say, "The doctor will see you now." This was followed by a laugh, a female laugh. Joan led in a woman. "This is Mr. Barrington. Mr. Barrington, this is Ms. Fiske."

Stone tried to focus on her and failed. The blur of her was tall and slim, though, and

8

that was a start.

"How do you do?" she asked in a low-pitched voice.

Stone felt as if he were Humphrey Bogart, meeting Lauren Bacall for the first time. "Very well, thank you," he said, struggling to his feet and extending a hand. "Won't you sit down?"

She shook his hand, then sat down across the desk from him and crossed her legs. "Thank you."

"Would you like some coffee?"

"You look as though you need it more than I," she said.

"There's enough for both of us."

"I've already had my morning coffee, and a second cup would just get me wired."

It was easier to focus on her sitting down, and, once he was able to focus, it was very pleasant, too. She had blond hair, parted on the right and held back by a tortoiseshell clip. "It's not working that way for me — not yet, anyway." He took another sip and didn't burn his tongue.

"You look jet-lagged."

"I am — thank you for not suggesting I have a hangover."

"You're welcome. Where have you flown in from?"

"The south of England."

"London?"

"Farther south — Hampshire."

"But you flew from London."

"No, from Hampshire."

"I didn't know you could do that — fly from Hampshire to New York."

"You can, but you have to fly the airplane yourself."

"And it would have to be a big enough airplane to have that kind of range."

"No, just big enough to make it to the Azores, then Newfoundland, then Teterboro."

"And how big is that?"

"You know Citations?"

"Yes, my former husband owned one, until the bank took it away from him."

"A Citation M2."

"Oh. I used to fly a Bonanza."

The conversation was cutting the fog, so he continued. "So did I — a B-36TC."

"Mine was an A36."

"Sweet airplane, isn't it?"

"It was. My husband made me sell it when we got married. He was afraid to fly with me."

"The swine."

"Now that you mention it, yes. He's why I'm here."

"Are you divorced?"

"Yes, almost a year ago."

"Did you get a satisfactory settlement?"

"No, but he did."

"Ah."

"Exactly."

"Does he want more?"

"Yes, but he knows he has no chance of that."

"Then what's the problem?"

"He won't leave me alone — he follows me, turns up at places I'm going."

"Does he bother you on those occasions?"

"Yes. Oh, he doesn't push me around or anything, he just stares at me unrelentingly."

"There's a word for that — stalking. And there's a very useful New York State law against it."

"Sure there is, but it won't do me any good when I'm dead."

"Has he threatened you?"

"He doesn't speak, he just stares."

"But you think he wants to kill you?"

"I know he does. He told me right after we were married that if I ever left him, he'd kill me. I have no reason to doubt him."

"How long were you married?"

"About five months, before I filed for divorce."

"And you've been divorced for nearly a year?"

"That's correct."

Stone took a big swig of the coffee; it was clearing his head. "Then why hasn't he killed you?"

"He just isn't ready yet. Harvey was always a planner. I don't think that has changed."

Stone took a yellow pad from a desk drawer and picked up a pen. "All right, let's start at the beginning. What is your name?"

"Carrie Jarman Fiske."

"Jarman?"

"My grandfather was in shoes — Jarman shoes."

"I see. Address?"

She gave him a very, very good Park Avenue address.

"Age?"

"That's rude."

"I'm guessing, forty . . ."

"Thirty-four."

"That was my first guess. Are you employed, Ms. Fiske?"

"Self-employed. I'm an investor."

"Any children?"

"None. I took precautions."

"What is your ex-husband's name?"

"Harvey Biggers."

"Is he employed?"

"Yes."

"What is his business?"

"Managing my money."

"Before that?"

"Managing other people's money."

"Was he successful at managing your money?"

"He would have been an abject failure if I had listened to him."

"Beg pardon? He didn't have control of your funds?"

"Certainly not. I may have been stupid to marry him, but I'm not crazy. He *thought* he managed my money, but he had no control of it. He would say, 'Sell Apple,' and I'd pretend to call my broker and tell him to sell Apple."

"So you never sold Apple?"

"Of course not. My grandfather left those shares to me, twenty-five thousand of them, also ten thousand shares of a very nice company called Berkshire Hathaway."

"Your grandfather was a good stock picker. How long ago did he leave you these shares?"

"He died when I was seven."

"You said he was in shoes?"

"He was a traveling salesman. He sold men's suits and shoes to stores all over the Southeast. But he was also a very good poker player, very shrewd. He played poker almost every night for forty years when he was on the road, and he banked his winnings. Then, once a month, he would invest them. The shares were put into a trust when he died, and I got control when I was twenty-five."

"And when you divorced, what did you have to give your husband?"

"A hundred thousand dollars."

"That was it?"

"Yep. I wrote him a check, moved his stuff out of my apartment, and told the doormen to call the police if he ever showed up."

"Did you have a restraining order against him?"

"Yes, one that prevents him from coming closer to me than a hundred feet, and he never has."

"So, you're legally divorced, your settlement was paid, and he hasn't violated the TRO?"

"That is correct."

"Then there's nothing we can do. Legally."

"How about illegally?"

"No, no, don't even think that. Do you have your ex-husband's address?"

She gave him the number of an apartment building on Second Avenue. "It's a studio," she said. "I suppose he's living frugally."

"Do you have a will?"

She blinked. "Yes. I forgot. And he's the sole heir. How could I forget that?" She slapped her forehead.

"Where is the original of the will?"

"It's in my safe, in my apartment."

"Well, when it's convenient, get it to me. In the meantime, let's draw up a new will."

"Right now?"

"The sooner the better," Stone said. "And we'll send your ex-husband a copy."

She glanced at her watch. "I can't do it right now; I have a lunch date."

"Don't delay."

"Don't worry."

2

"Now," Stone said, "do you mind having some company for a few days?"

"Are you volunteering?" she asked, a little smile on her face.

"I'm volunteering a man who works for me. His name is Fred Flicker, and he is very competent."

"And what will his duties be?"

"To see that you move about safely, and to frighten your ex-husband."

"Harvey was a boxing champion at Yale," she said. "He doesn't frighten easily."

"He hasn't met Fred Flicker. Shall I introduce you?"

"All right."

Stone buzzed Joan. "Please ask Fred to join us." He hung up the phone. "He'll be just a moment."

A moment later Fred Flicker entered the room. "You rang, sir?" Fred Flicker would have been about five-six, if he wore heels, which he did not.

"I did, Fred. This is Ms. Fiske. I would like you to accompany her everywhere she goes for the next few days. Her ex-husband has been following her, and when given the opportunity, I would like you to persuade him to discontinue that activity."

"How much persuasion may I use, sir?"

"You may not harm him, except in self-defense."

"Will he be armed?"

Stone looked at Carrie and raised his eyebrows.

"He owns guns," she said. "I don't know if he has been walking around armed."

"Does he have a license to do so?"

"I'm not sure."

"I expect not. Do you mind if he is sent to prison for a while?"

"For killing me? For a very long time, please."

"No, for carrying a gun illegally."

"Sure, why not?"

"Fred, if you learn that Mr. Harvey Biggers — that's his name — is carrying, take steps."

"Quite, sir."

"You may go and get the car, Fred. Ms. Fiske will meet you outside momentarily."

Fred disappeared.

"You really think this is going to work?" she asked.

"Very probably. Bullies don't like being confronted by those they have not chosen to bully."

"Harvey is a bully, now that you mention it, but I'm not sure that little man will frighten him."

"That little man, as you describe him, is a retired regimental sergeant of the Royal Marine Commandos. He is extraordinarily well qualified to frighten bullies."

"I can't wait to see this."

"Then go somewhere today where you think Harvey might follow you. Fred is waiting outside in my car. I would like him to drive you anywhere you wish to go."

"For how long?"

"Until Harvey vanishes."

"Well," she said, getting to her feet, "I guess this is worth a try. What do we do if it doesn't work?"

"We'll cross that gutter when we come to it." Stone shook her hand, and she left his office. He heard the outside door close behind her.

Joan came in. "What was she about?"

"About an ex-husband who won't leave her alone."

"Oh, one of those."

"Yes, one of those."

"You seem to have known a number of women with ex-husbands or boyfriends like that."

"It has been my lot in life to know such women."

"You attract them the way other people attract mosquitoes. How did you attract this one?"

"I forgot to ask her who recommended me."

"She reminds me of a young Lauren Bacall."

"Me too."

"Don't start thinking you're Humphrey Bogart," she said, then went back to her desk. A moment later she buzzed him. "Dino on one."

Stone picked up the phone. "Good morning," he said.

"It's not bad," Dino replied. Back when Stone had been an NYPD detective, he and Dino had been partners. Dino had prospered and was now the New York City police commissioner.

"I wish I could say that," Stone said. "I woke up feeling like one of the undead. Funny, though, I feel better now."

"How'd you get over that? It's too early in the morning for you to have met a new woman."

"Actually," Stone said, "it's not."

3

Fred Flicker had a good look at Ms. Fiske as he held open the door of the Bentley. Pretty good, he thought, but Fred was a harsh judge of flesh. He got into the driver's seat.

"And where would you like to go, madam?" he asked.

"Madam? Really?"

"Would you prefer miss?"

"Infinitely."

"Where would you like to go, miss?"

"Home?"

"Would you like to give me a hint?"

"Oh, I'm sorry — 740 Park Avenue."

"Yes, miss." Fred put the car in gear and drove away. Fifteen minutes later he pulled to a stop in front of her building, got out and opened the door for her.

"Thank you, Fred."

He handed her a card. "Please call me at this number when you're ready to go out, miss. I'll be here in five minutes."

"Actually," she said, "I'd rather just go to lunch now. I'm presentable, no need to go upstairs." She got back into the car.

Fred mounted the driver's seat again. "Where to, miss?"

"The Boathouse in Central Park," she said, dialing a number on her cell phone.

"Yes, miss." Ten minutes later they were there. Fred assisted her from the car, then parked it and followed her into the restaurant. She was seated at an outside table overlooking the lake. A woman entered, they air-kissed, and the two women sat down together.

Fred stood to one side of the seating area and was approached by the headwaiter.

"May I help you?" the man asked, in a tone that sounded as if he had no wish to help.

"Security," Fred said, nodding toward the Fiske table.

"Really?"

"Really. Trust me."

"Oh, all right." He stalked away.

A moment later the waiter returned to the terrace, leading a large, handsome gentleman. Fred looked him over: six-five, maybe six-six, two-twenty, chiseled features, square jaw. He was seated on the opposite side of the outdoor area from where Ms. Fiske sat. He looked at her, she looked at the man and nodded.

Fred walked over to the man's table. "Good afternoon," he said.

The man looked at him disdainfully. "Is it?"

"Take my word for it," Fred replied. "I am a security person for Ms. Fiske."

The man looked him up and down. "Really?"

"Really. She would be very grateful if you would leave the restaurant and not follow her anywhere again."

The man stood up and approached Fred, who remained rooted to the spot. He reached out, put his hands under Fred's arms and lifted him like a child, until they were nose to nose. "I would be very grateful if you would go away and stay away," he said.

Fred reached out with both hands and briefly explored the man's rib cage. Gun under the left armpit. "Kindly put me down and take your hands away," he said.

"Or what?"

"Or I'll hurt you."

Broad smile. "I'd like to see you try."

Fred reached out with both hands, took the man by his ears and head-butted him squarely in the nose, hard. The man dropped him, and Fred landed on his toes. The man clapped a hand over his nose, and blood seeped between his fingers. Fred picked up a napkin from the table and handed it to him. "Use this," he said, "and if I were you I'd run over to the nearest emergency room and have that nose looked at. It will need setting." While Fred waited for a reply, the headwaiter appeared again, this time in the company of two uniformed police officers.

"Can you do something about this, please?" he said, indicating Fred.

"Okay, what's happening here?" one of the cops said.

"This man assaulted me," Fred replied evenly. "It was necessary for me to defend myself."

The cop removed the man's hand from his face and took a look at his nose, then he turned to Fred. "You did that? How'd you reach that high?"

"He lifted me into range," Fred replied. "And I have reason to believe that he is armed — shoulder holster, left side."

"Oh, yeah?" The cop patted the area, then reached inside the man's jacket and pulled out a small 9mm pistol. "Tell you what," he said. "We'll give you a lift to the ER, and on

the way we can have a little chat about this."
He held up the gun.

The man nodded, and the two policemen escorted him from the restaurant. Fred walked over to Ms. Fiske's table. "I don't believe he'll bother you for the remainder of the day, miss."

"I'm so glad," Ms. Fiske replied. "In that case, I don't believe I'll need you for the rest of the day, Fred. You may convey the news to Mr. Barrington."

"I will do so, miss," Fred replied. "Good day." He walked out of the restaurant and went for the car.

Half an hour later, Fred had conveyed the news to Mr. Barrington.

"Well done," Stone said.

"Thank you, sir."

"Do you think he got the message?"

"If he didn't, next time I'll break his patella — that will keep him out of action for a while."

"As long as it's in self-defense," Stone said, and Fred took his leave.

Stone joined Dino and his wife, Viv, for dinner at Patroon that evening, and he told them about Fred's actions that afternoon.

"Sounds like a law-abiding citizen to me," Dino said.

"Fred or the other guy?"

"Fred, of course. It would have weighed with the arresting officer that he was so much smaller than the one who was doing the bleeding. What was this all about?"

"Recently divorced woman with an ex-husband who can't face reality and is stalking her."

Dino, to Stone's astonishment, began to sing: "It seems to me I've heard that song before. It's from an old familiar score . . ."

"Dino," Viv said. "I never knew you could sing."

"He can't," Stone replied.

"Still, the song resonates, doesn't it?" Dino asked. "Jule Styne and Sammy Cahn."

"I'll bet you didn't know he was a musicologist, either," Stone said to Viv.

"I learn something new about him every . . . month or so," she replied.

"Half the women Stone has ever been involved with had angry men in the way."

"I'm not involved with her," Stone said, "she's a client."

"That never got in the way before, and I don't think the American Bar Association would like it."

"So, I offer some of my clients a broad range of services."

26

Viv burst out laughing. "Don't tell me, just let my imagination run wild."

4

Stone was at his desk the following morning when he heard voices — a man and a woman — followed by scuffling sounds, followed by a very large man with a length of tape across his nose and two black eyes, looking much like a sorrowful raccoon. Right behind him was Joan, wielding the .45 that she kept in her desk drawer.

"Freeze!" she yelled.

"Joan!" Stone said loudly. "Don't shoot him!"

"Oh, all right," Joan replied, sounding disappointed. She lowered the weapon.

"Who are you and what do you want?" Stone asked. "And talk fast, or I'll let her shoot you."

"My name is Harvey Biggers," the man said.

"Oh, right. Sorry, I was a little slow on the uptake. You'd better sit down before you pass out. I'll handle this, Joan. Put the gun away."

Biggers sat down. "I have to talk to you."

"I'm afraid that conversation can't take place," Stone said, "since I represent your former wife."

"Look, you don't know what you're getting mixed up in. Don't worry, I won't ask you for legal advice. Just give me five minutes to ease my conscience."

"Your conscience? If you want to confess, speak to somebody at the Nineteenth Precinct."

"This is not a confession, it's a warning."

"A warning about what?"

"About what you're getting mixed up in."

"Mr. Biggers, every time I take on a client I get mixed up in something, it's what I do. Now what's your point?"

"You've been misled."

"Not for the first time."

"Maybe not, but this time could be fatal."

"Fatal for whom?"

"For you. Sorry, that was a terrible joke. Fatal for me, actually."

Stone sighed deeply. "You're not making any sense at all, Mr. Biggers."

"I'm being set up."

"Set up for what?"

"For getting killed."

"Let me give you a little help with the noir

nomenclature, Mr. Biggers. When you're being set up it means someone is trying to have you wrongly accused of killing someone else."

"It does?"

"Yes."

"Can't it mean something else, too?"

"What did you have in mind?"

"For someone else killing me?"

"Ah, you mean being set up to *be* killed?"

"That's what I said."

"That may be what you were trying to say, but it didn't come out that way. You mean, someone is trying to kill you?"

"Not yet."

"When?"

"Very soon, it seems."

"Who is trying to kill you?"

"Not trying, planning."

"All right, who is planning to kill you?"

"My wife, of course."

"Mr. Biggers, do you have more than one wife?"

"Well, not at a time. But right now I have two ex-wives, and one of them is trying to kill me."

"Which one?"

"Why, your client, of course."

"Mr. Biggers, unless you start making some sense real quick, the lady with the gun in the outside office is going to come back, and my client will never have the chance to kill you."

"I know you will find this hard to believe, but she wants you to believe that I am trying to kill her, when it is she who wants to kill me. Look at me, she's already gotten me beat up."

"No, you got yourself beat up when you assaulted my associate, Fred."

"That little twerp is your associate?"

"Mr. Biggers, let me remind you that the man you are referring to as 'that little twerp' put you in the hospital and made you look like a raccoon."

"He just got lucky that time."

"No, in that regard he is always lucky, and you should not provoke him again into having to defend himself. Now can we get back to the point?"

"The point is that your client, Carrie Fiske, wants you to think I want to kill her, when in reality it is she who wants to kill me."

"Mr. Biggers, while I appreciate your newfound clarity of thought, your thought is preposterous. Why would she want to kill you?"

"Because she's mad at me, and because she's mean."

"Let's take those one at a time. Why is she mad at you?"

"Because I left her. Isn't 'Hell hath no fury like a woman scorned' a motive in this modern world?"

"I'll grant you that — a woman scorned is capable of a lot."

"Carrie is capable of *anything.*"

"All right, how is she mean?"

"In any way you can possibly think of — she's mean morning, noon, and night, especially at night, in bed."

Stone wanted to rest his forehead on the glass top of his desk and cool his fevered brow, but instead he did the right thing. "Mr. Biggers," he said, "I cannot listen to your concerns any longer. I refer you to the New York City Police Department, to which you can express your fears and even make a charge against Ms. Fiske, should you desire to do so. Now, this conversation is at an end. Please leave before I ask my secretary to escort you from the premises with a .45 stuck in your ribs."

Harvey Biggers made a small noise, then he got up and strode, nearly ran, from Stone's office. Stone heard the outside door close.

Joan came into his office. "Did he harm you?"

"No, he was too afraid of you."

5

Biggers had not been gone five minutes when Joan buzzed.

"Carrie Fiske on line one."

Stone pressed the button. "Hello, Carrie."

"Hello, Stone."

"I hope you are well."

"So far. Tell me, have you heard from my ex-husband?"

"Yes, and from close range."

"What does that mean?"

"It means he was right across my desk."

"In your office?"

"That's where my desk is."

"Good God! Did he hurt you?"

"I don't think he is in any shape to hurt anybody today — he just got out of the hospital."

"I saw what Fred did to him. That little man was magnificent. Who knew?"

"I knew — your ex-husband didn't. He does now, though."

"What did he want?"

"He wanted me to know that you are trying to kill him."

"What nonsense! Why would I want to kill him?"

"That's what I asked him."

"And what did he say?"

"He said, because you're mad at him, and you're mean, especially in bed."

"Well, God knows, I'm mad at him for creating that scene at the Central Park Boathouse. But mean? And in bed? What did he mean by that?"

"I was afraid to ask."

"That's very odd. I don't think anyone has ever said I was mean in bed."

"It is certainly odd, and I'm relieved to hear that you don't have that reputation."

"I wouldn't like for a charge like that to get around — it might damage my . . . social life."

"No doubt."

"Can I sue him for defamation?"

"That is inadvisable."

"But he has defamed me."

"I don't doubt that, but in the legal process of suing him . . ."

"Yes? Go on."

"Well, do you remember that woman who was known as the Queen of Mean?"

"Leona Helmsley?"

"That's the one."

"What does she have to do with it?"

"I fear that, at least in the *New York Post*, you might well find yourself billed as the Queen of Mean in Bed, thus defeating the purpose of your lawsuit and sticking you with that sobriquet for life, perhaps longer."

"Longer?"

"It might end up on your tombstone."

"How?"

"You said you had a will. In it, is the person in charge of your funeral arrangements your husband?"

"Oh, shit."

"Exactly. I think we need to draw up a new will for you right away, especially since you think he wants to kill you. If he managed to do that, and get away with it, he would be in charge of everything."

"Why don't you come out to my house in the Hamptons for the weekend?" she said, abruptly changing the subject.

Stone reflected that he had no plans for the weekend, but still . . .

"And," she added before he could speak, "I have some friends coming that you might enjoy. And you could draw up my new will, before Harvey gets a chance to kill me."

"You make a weekend in the Hamptons

sound like an emergency."

"A dire emergency. Do you know Georgica Pond?"

"I know that it's a very nice neighborhood. I read the real estate ads in the Sunday *Times* magazine."

"Can you find it?"

"Probably not, but the GPS lady in my car can."

She gave him the address. "Lunch is at one o'clock tomorrow. Be there in time for the world's best Bloody Mary."

"I don't drink before noon."

"That's why lunch is at one. And bring a dinner jacket."

"To the Hamptons? I haven't spent a lot of time out there, but my impression is that everybody is terribly, terribly casual."

"Do you own a dinner jacket?"

"I do."

"Bring it," she said.

"Yes, ma'am," he replied.

"That's better." She hung up.

6

Stone thought about flying to the East Hampton airport, but he knew he would have to avoid Kennedy and LaGuardia airports and that the route might be too circuitous. Instead, he got out the Blaise, a French sports car built by his friend Marcel duBois. He had not driven it enough; the odometer showed less than a thousand miles.

He put his luggage into the small trunk and backed slowly out of the garage, using the remote to close the door. Half an hour later he was sorry he hadn't flown. Once through the Midtown Tunnel and out of the city, he found himself in bumper-to-bumper traffic, moving at an average speed of about thirty miles an hour. At least he was moving.

Finally, the lady in his navigation system, who charmingly spoke with a French accent, guided him into East Hampton village and out to Georgica Pond, to the front door of a handsome, shingle-style house of some size, where the Blaise shared parking with two Porsches and a Mercedes. A yellow Labrador retriever bounded out of the house, first barking, then allowing Stone to scratch his back.

Carrie Fiske stuck her head out the door and shouted, "Leave your luggage. Rupert will take it to your room and unpack for you!" Stone left the trunk open for Rupert and went inside, the Lab staying at his knee all the way, tail wagging.

Carrie allowed herself to be kissed on both cheeks. "Don't mind Bob," she said, indicating the dog. "If he annoys you, just tell him, 'Go away.' They were among the first words he learned."

"He's not annoying me," Stone said. "I haven't had this much attention for a long time."

Carrie led him into the living room and introduced him to two other couples. "This is Nicky and Vanessa Chalmers," she said, indicating two handsome people lounging on a white sofa, "and that's Derek and Alicia Bedford. This is Stone Barrington." Two people in armchairs gave a limp wave. Nobody got up to greet him; apparently that was Bob's job.

"You're half an hour late," Carrie said. "I know — traffic. Those of us who live out here depart the city at dawn or midnight to miss it, visitors get bogged down in it."

"Count me among the latter."

A man in a white jacket, apparently Rupert, appeared with a silver tray bearing a large glass of a blood-red liquid with several kinds of vegetables crowding the top. Stone located a straw among the vegetation and drew a long sip. "That's the best Bloody Mary I've ever tasted," he said. "What's your secret?"

"The secret is Rupert's, and he's not telling, are you, Rupert?"

"No, madam," Rupert replied in a crisp British accent.

"So you see why I can't fire him."

"I see," Stone replied. "That would be unwise."

"I know a dozen people out here who would hire Rupert away, just for his Bloody Marys."

"I'm sure he has other gifts, as well," Stone said.

"Thank you, Mr. Barrington," Rupert said, and left the room. A moment later Stone heard his trunk lid slam, and he winced. Then Rupert ran lightly up the stairs carrying Stone's cases. He appeared to be in very good shape.

"So, Stone," Nicky drawled in a New England Lockjaw accent, "who are you? I've never heard of you."

"Millions haven't," Stone replied.

"I can't place your accent."

"I don't think I have one. Sorry, I don't mean to be difficult."

"Stone is my new lawyer," Carrie said. "He's come all the way out here to write me a new will."

"I doubt that," Vanessa said, in a duplicate of Nicky's accent. "He looks to me as though he has ulterior motives." She turned to Carrie. "Or is that you sending that vibe?"

"Be nice, Vanessa, or Stone will think you're a bitch. You too, Nicky."

"Me, a bitch? Well, I never."

"You do all the time," Carrie replied. "And you know it. You're just suspicious of people who have jobs."

"Well, working does seem an awful waste of time, doesn't it? I don't know why anyone does it."

Stone wanted to go to the fireplace, find the poker, and wrap it around his neck.

"Almost everyone does, Nicky," Carrie said. "Even the one-tenth of one percent, like you. But not even they have a trust fund the size of yours." She turned toward Stone.

"Nicky's great-grandfather founded one of America's first tire companies more than a century ago, just at the moment when his product became a necessity."

"You chose your ancestors well," Stone said to him.

Nicky beamed at the thought.

They were at lunch on the rear deck, going at a lobster salad and drinking Montrachet, when Nicky started in again.

"So, Stone, let's talk real estate. Where do you live?"

"In New York, you mean?"

"Oh, everywhere — tell us all."

"In New York, I live in Turtle Bay. I also have homes in Dark Harbor, on Islesboro, in Maine, in Paris, and in Los Angeles. And I recently acquired a property in the south of England."

"My, my, you do get around."

"I get the feeling, Nicky," Derek said, speaking for the first time, "that you're dying to tell us where *you* live."

"Oh, only in Greenwich, Manhattan, and Palm Beach," Nicky replied. "I'm practically homeless, compared to Stone."

That got a laugh.

"I would be interested to know," Carrie said, "how and why you acquired each of those properties, Stone. If I'm not prying."

"Well, let's see. I inherited the house in Turtle Bay from a great-aunt, many years ago, when I was a police officer. Renovating it nearly broke me, so I took up the law to pay for the renovation and the property taxes."

"A police officer!" Nicky cried. "I want to hear about that."

"A much longer story," Stone said.

"And Maine?"

"A first cousin left it to me after his untimely death, or rather, left me lifetime occupancy. I later bought it from the foundation that held title."

"Aren't you fortunate?" Carrie said. "Such nice relatives. Did you have an uncle in Los Angeles?"

"I'm a principal in a group of hotels, the first of which was built on property in Bel-Air owned by my late wife."

"Ah, another inheritance!" Nicky crowed. "It's better than a trust fund!"

"Paris?" Carrie persisted.

"I spent some time in a house owned by . . . an acquaintance, and I ended up buying it."

"Where in Paris?"

"Saint-Germain-des-Prés."

"Lovely. That leaves only the south of

England."

"A friend showed me a property on the Beaulieu River, near her home. She said I'd be taken with it, and she was right."

Stone tried redirecting the conversation. "Derek, what do you do?"

"Oh, this and that," Derek said. "I buy and sell."

"Buy and sell what?"

Carrie interrupted. "Jewelry, mostly. Derek has the best eye for quality that I've ever known."

"You're too kind, Carrie," Derek said.

"Not in the least!" she replied. "I've got three generations of jewelry in my safe, and Derek is going to help me cull the most out-of-date pieces and get the most money for them."

Derek looked embarrassed. "I'll do the best I can, Carrie, when you deign to show me the contents of that safe."

Then, with complete suddenness, the conversation came to a halt. The wind had apparently shifted.

"Good God," Carrie said, "what is that awful odor?"

Bob, who had been lying quietly at Stone's feet, got up, jumped down from the deck, and began trotting in the direction of the next property.

Stone knew what the odor was. "Excuse me," he said.

He got up and followed Bob.

7

Bob trotted toward the twelve-foot-high hedge that separated Carrie's house from the next property, and hardly slowed as he squirmed through a hole at the bottom of the greenery. Stone took a right and walked to where the hedge parted to accommodate a padlocked gate. Stone grabbed the top of the gate and vaulted over.

Bob was sitting on the grass at the end of the house, looking at a pair of open windows on the second floor. He tilted his head back, aimed at the sky and gave forth with a single, long howl, then he came to Stone and sat down. "Thank you, Bob," Stone said. "Message received. Let's go have a look."

Stone climbed the curving front steps to the porch and rang the doorbell. He could hear the chime from somewhere deep inside. He hammered on the front door, then tried opening it. To his surprise, unlike the front gate, it was unlocked. The odor got stronger. "Hello!" he shouted. "Anyone home?" He started to look around the ground floor, but Bob trotted up the stairs. Stone followed and came to a long hallway. Bob was sitting at the end in front of a closed door, looking back at him and whimpering. Stone walked down the hall and rapped on the door. "Hello! Anybody there?" He opened the door; the stench was overpowering. Bob entered, ran across the room and sat down next to the king-sized bed. There were women's clothes in the closet and shoes scattered around the room. Stone tried breathing through a handkerchief. The bed was covered by a large duvet, and there was a large lump beneath it.

He took a deep breath and pulled back the duvet, just for a second. He didn't need more than that to know that he didn't want to see any more of what was there. He returned the duvet to its original position and left the room. "Come on, Bob," he said, and the dog followed him. He closed the door behind him and walked down the hallway. He could hear voices from downstairs now.

His five luncheon companions were standing in the living room, chatting quietly and looking around.

"Did you find anything?" Carrie asked.

Stone didn't reply; he didn't want to explain more than once. He got out his iPhone and dialed 911.

"Nine-one-one, what is your emergency?" a woman said.

"Please connect me with the watch commander."

"What is your emergency?"

"I'm going to explain it only once, and to him. Give me your watch commander now, or I'll come over there."

"Please hold."

The extension rang half a dozen times, and finally a man answered. "This is Sergeant D'Orio. What can I do for you?"

Stone gave him the address. "My name is Stone Barrington. I'm a retired NYPD detective. I'm a guest at the house next door, and I detected a powerful odor coming from this house, so I investigated. No one answered the door, but it was unlocked, so I went inside. I found the remains of a woman — at least I think it's a woman — in an upstairs bedroom, in an advanced state of decay. I'll wait for your team to arrive. You're going to need a crime-scene specialist and the medical examiner, also some bolt cutters. The front gate is padlocked."

"All right. Don't touch anything in the house. We're on our way."

"I don't think the neighbors would appreciate lights and sirens," Stone said. "The person upstairs isn't going anywhere, so take your time."

"Right. Sit tight." He hung up, and so did Stone. He addressed the little group in the living room. "Unless you want to spend a long afternoon answering the same questions over and over, you should all go back to the house now, before the police arrive, and Carrie, please take Bob with you. Did anybody touch anything?"

They all shook their heads.

"I'll come back as soon as I can."

"All right, everybody, let's go home. Come on, Bob."

"By the way, Carrie, who owns this house?"

"A friend of my ex-husband," she replied. "His name is James Carlton."

"Film director?"

"That's the one. The place is for sale."

"I didn't see a real estate agent's sign."

"The people around here don't like signs in their yards. Join us for cocktails, if you can. Dinner is at seven-thirty, and we're dressing."

Stone nodded, and she left. He took a seat

on the living room sofa. A moment later Stone heard a snap from outside and the creak of the opening gate. Car doors slammed, and there were footsteps on the outside stairs.

A chunky police sergeant walked into the house and stopped. "Are you Barrington?"

"I am," Stone said, rising to greet him.

"I'm Dante D'Orio," he said, offering his hand.

Stone shook it. "Have a seat, and I'll bring you up to date."

D'Orio took the chair opposite and prepared to listen.

When Stone had finished, he asked, "Do you know who owns this house?"

"I'm told James Carlton."

"The movie guy?"

"Yes. Apparently the house is on the market."

"Do you know how long it's been since anybody was here?"

"No, but you'd think that some real estate people might have been in here. The place isn't exactly in a condition to show."

Other people began to arrive, some of them carrying cases and equipment.

"You'll have to excuse me," D'Orio said.

"Do you need me further?"

"I'd like to know how to get in touch with you."

Stone wrote his cell number on a card and handed it to him. "I'll be next door at the home of Carrie Fiske if you need me."

Stone returned to the house next door.

8

Stone dressed in a white dinner jacket and joined the others downstairs for cocktails; everybody was one drink ahead of him. To his pleasant surprise, Rupert was able to come up with a Knob Creek on the rocks.

"So, Stone," Nicky said, "what did the police have to say?"

"I did most of the talking," Stone said, "just telling them what I had seen. They went to work, and I left."

"What did you see upstairs?" Nicky asked.

"Our worst fears realized."

"Details?"

"I wouldn't want to ruin your canapés."

"That bad, huh?"

"As bad as it gets."

"Man or woman?"

"A woman, judging from the clothes in the room. Otherwise, it was hard to tell. Something I don't understand — if the house is on the market, why haven't there been real estate people in there, showing it?"

"Jim is asking thirty-five million," Carrie said. "That tends to cut down on the foot traffic."

"I suppose so. Do you know when he was last here?"

"I keep my house open year-round," she said. "I haven't seen him since Christmas. I read somewhere that he was making a film in London — maybe he hasn't returned for a while."

"Do you know who the agents are?"

"Best Hamptons Properties, Julia Fields. I saw her arrive with some people — buyers, I guess — right after New Year's. Nobody since. Do you think the body has been there that long?"

"Bodies decay at different rates, depending on the conditions present. I'm not an expert. When I was a cop I usually saw them when they were still fresh, with a few exceptions. I've tried to forget those."

"How did you go from being a cop to being a lawyer?" Nicky asked.

"My senior year at NYU Law School I did a ride-around with the police, and I was captivated. After I graduated, I joined the NYPD. I was invalided out fourteen years later, after getting shot in a knee, and I happened to bump into a law school classmate who suggested I take a cram course for the bar exam, then become of counsel to his firm."

"What's 'of counsel'?"

"It just means you're not a partner or an associate. In my case it meant that I handled cases that the firm didn't want to be seen as handling, often things that related to my experience as a police detective."

"I'd like to read a book about those cases," Carrie said.

"It will never be published, unless it's without my knowledge. Your turn on the grill, Nicky," Stone said. "Where'd you go to school?"

"Groton and Yale, art history major."

"That qualifies you to be a dealer, I guess."

"It sort of qualifies me to be a collector. I've never had a job. I shouldn't say that too loudly, in case my great-grandfather is listening from somewhere. From what I know of him, it wouldn't please him. Actually, over the years I've sold at a profit often enough to qualify as having made a living, if not quite the living that my trust has paid for."

"I should think not," Carrie said. "And Nicky, when you were confessing your real estate sins, you forgot to include the house in the South of France."

"Oh, yes, that one. You've caught me. Stone, I'm interested in your property in the south of England. What does it consist of?"

"Eighty acres and a Georgian-style manor house, built in the twenties."

"What attracted you to it?"

"It's quite beautiful. It had just undergone a thorough renovation by a good designer, and it's on a beautiful river with easy access to the Solent, the body of water that separates the mainland from the Isle of Wight. I sail now and then. What attracted you to Palm Beach?"

"I inherited the house, and nobody would buy it."

Everybody laughed. "Donald Trump tried, before he bought his present property, but Nicky was too much of a snob to sell it to him."

"That's quite true," Nicky said. "I was and *am* a snob. I'm attracted to people of substance, not just money. What is the name of the law firm to which you are 'of counsel,' Stone?"

"Woodman & Weld. I'm a partner these days."

"An estimable firm."

"Thank you."

"Was your law school friend Bill Eggers?"

"He was and is."

"I knew him as a Yale undergrad. May I call you next week? I'm not entirely satisfied with my representation."

"Of course." Stone handed him a card. "I visit the office from time to time, but I mostly work out of my home. Come and see me there."

Nicky pocketed the card. "I'll do that."

Rupert materialized. "Dinner is served, madam."

And they went in.

When they came out, Sergeant D'Orio was waiting for Stone. They went out onto the deck and took a seat. It was a balmy night, with a moon rising.

"You've been a cop," D'Orio said, "so you'll understand the reason for these questions."

"Of course."

"When did you arrive out here?"

"About one-thirty this afternoon, in time for a Bloody Mary and lunch. Our meal was interrupted when the wind changed."

"When were you last in the Hamptons?"

"The summer before last, in June, I believe."

"Account for your movements for the past three months."

"I spent about three weeks in Rome in the early spring, then flew to England, where I bought a house and some property. I remained there until last weekend, when I flew back."

"What airline did you take?"

"I took Alitalia to Rome, then my airplane was ferried over. I flew to England and then to Teterboro, New Jersey, in that aircraft."

"Who flew with you?"

"I was alone, but the people at the hangar at Jet Aviation belonging to Strategic Services can confirm when I landed. You can also search the aviation databases for my flight plans."

"Have you ever met Darla Henry?"

"Who's that?"

"If the tags on the luggage in the room are to be believed, she was the lady on the bed."

"I've never met her and never heard that name. Incidentally, my hostess, who keeps her house open year-round, has not seen James Carlton since he spent the Christmas holiday at his house. I understand he's in London, making a film."

"That coincides with what the real estate agency had to say."

"Have you spoken to Carlton?"

"I've left two messages with his production company at Pinewood Studios, in England. I haven't heard back."

"What did your ME have to say about the remains?"

"He puts the time of death at ten to twelve weeks, but he doesn't have a cause of death yet. He said there was no evidence of a gunshot, stabbing, or strangulation. That doesn't mean that something might not turn up after further analysis."

"Drugs?"

"We found a bottle containing a sleeping pill, Ambien, on the bedside table, with two remaining tablets. We'll have to wait for a tox screen to know if she took any, and that will take weeks."

"What have you learned about Darla Henry?"

"She has a Florida driver's license with a West Palm Beach address — a rental apartment — and she moved out early in the year and left no forwarding address. A lot of her clothes had Bloomingdale's labels, with a few from Palm Beach." He handed Stone the license, showing a pretty blonde of thirty-three.

"I've never seen her," Stone said. "The clothing labels make it sound like she spent some time in New York."

"Can I speak to your dinner partners?"

Stone shrugged. "Okay with me, but I think the four guests arrived earlier today, and my hostess, I think, would have told me more if she knew anything. I'm also her attorney."

"A long relationship?"

"She hired me a couple of days ago. I'll be drawing a will for her tomorrow. She's recently divorced and needs to make some changes."

"Sounds like a dry hole for me," D'Orio said.

"Probably. Did you ask the realtor if anyone has rented the house since Christmas?"

"Yes, and no one has."

"Perhaps Ms. Henry is a friend of James Carlton."

"That's one of the things I'd like to ask him when he returns my calls." The cop stood up and offered his hand. "Thanks for your cooperation. I'll be in touch if I have any further questions."

"You've got my number."

9

The following morning Stone handed Carrie her new will. "Please have a look at that and tell me if there's anything you'd like changed."

She put the will in her handbag. "I'll read it when I get back to the city, I promise."

"Well, I could have saved a trip to East Hampton, then."

"I'm glad you didn't."

"I'm glad, too. Except for the unpleasantness next door, I'm enjoying myself."

"At least the odor went away."

"It left with the remains and the bed."

"I expect that will make it easier to sell the house."

"Maybe not. The story will make the local papers, and a lot of people won't want to buy a house that recently hosted a deteriorating corpse."

"I suppose not. Bob's happier, though."

"Bob would make a good investigator."

"He's certainly taken to you. He ignores everyone but Rupert, who feeds him, of course, but even they are not very good friends. Are you particularly good with dogs?"

"I've never owned one, but I've always gotten along with them."

"Feel like some tennis?" she asked. "Nicky and Vanessa are very good, and I'm all right."

"I didn't bring the gear."

"I think I can outfit you from the guest bin."

They played three sets, then showered before lunch.

They had just sat down when a distant phone rang, and Rupert came into the kitchen. "Excuse me, madam, but there's a Mr. James Carlton on the phone from London."

"Oh, dear," Carrie said. "You lot start eating while I speak to the man." She left the room. Five minutes later she came back. "Stone, Jim wants to speak with you."

Stone followed Rupert to a phone in the study. "Hello?"

"Mr. Barrington, this is Jim Carlton."

"How do you do?"

"Not so well, after what Carrie has just told me."

"Have you spoken to the East Hampton police?"

"Not yet. I wanted to know what was going on before I called them. Carrie said you could bring me up to date."

Stone gave him an account of events.

"Carrie says you're an attorney with a good New York firm."

"That's correct."

"I'd like to retain you to handle this for me."

"My guess is there's not a lot to handle, unless Ms. Henry was your guest."

"She was not, and I've never heard of her."

"Then I think you should call Sergeant D'Orio, listen to what he has to say, answer his questions, and if you're uncomfortable, tell him to speak to me."

"I'd rather you did that," Carlton said.

"All right, I'll represent you. I'll need some phone numbers." He noted the numbers. "Now, I have some questions."

"All right."

"When were you last at your East Hampton home?"

"At Christmastime. I threw a party on New Year's Eve and left for London on New Year's Day, and I can supply a list of guests, if he wants it. I've been here ever since."

"When will your business in London be

concluded?"

"As soon as we have a rough cut, then I'll go back to L.A. and finish up at the studio."

"Which studio?"

"Centurion."

"My son is based there — Peter Barrington."

"Oh, yes, I've met him a couple of times, but I don't know him well. I like his work, though."

"Have you rented out your house to anyone this year?"

"No, as far as I know it's been empty since I came to London."

"Do you think Ms. Henry might be a squatter?"

"Not unless she has a key and the security code."

"The house was unlocked when I was there, and the security system had apparently not been set."

"Then I'm baffled."

"All right, Mr. Carlton —"

"Jim."

"All right, Jim, I'll speak to the police and get back to you."

"I'm at a country inn this weekend. Call me tomorrow at the Pinewood number."

"Right. Can you e-mail me the party list?" He gave him the address, said goodbye, hung up, then returned to lunch.

"Are you representing Jim?" Carrie asked.

"Yes. I've acquired more new business this weekend than I know what to do with."

"You're welcome to stay on, if you need time to deal with this."

"Thank you. I think I'll need tomorrow, at least."

10

The following morning Stone got another call from James Carlton.

"I've decided to come back to the States tomorrow, and I'll spend the night at the house and speak to the police, if you want me to."

"I think that's a good idea."

"Is there any problem with cleaning the house before I get there? I have a service."

"I don't think so, but have them speak to me before they clean the room in question. I'll need to run that by the police first."

"Does the house stink?"

"Not anymore."

"Okay, I'll get it done. I should be at the house by about four o'clock tomorrow afternoon. I'll call you then. By the way, the party list is on my computer there, and I'll give it to you when I see you."

Both men said goodbye and hung up.

■ ■ ■ ■

After lunch Rupert loaded the cars of the two visiting couples.

"I'll call you in New York later this week," Nicky said to Stone.

"I'll look forward to hearing from you." The couples left in a Porsche and a Mercedes.

Carrie and Stone had a Bloody Mary before lunch, then Rupert served sandwiches. When he had cleared the table, Carrie gave him the rest of the day off, after he had supplied them with one more Bloody Mary.

They sat on a sofa, looking out over Georgica Pond and the Atlantic beyond. Carrie looked him in the eye. "The air feels so good, why don't we get out of these clothes?"

"Is that the Bloody Mary talking?"

"It's the Bloody Mary loosening my tongue," she said, then began to unbutton his shirt. He helped her out of her sweater and unfastened her bra, and in a moment they were sitting naked, staring at each other.

Stone looked her up and down. "You're beautiful."

"So are you," she said, stretching out on the big sofa and pulling his head down into her lap. "I just know you're going to be good at this."

Stone did the best he could, which by the sound of her was pretty good, then she reciprocated. They spent an hour exploring each other, then stretched out in each other's arms.

Stone was asleep when he heard a woman's voice call out, "Hello? Anybody home?"

Carrie poked her head above the back of the sofa and pushed Stone's down. "Who's that?"

"It's Julia, the realtor."

"I was having a nap, Julia. What can I do for you?"

"I wanted to have a look around next door, but there's yellow tape across the gate."

"The one that says 'Police Line Do Not Cross'?"

"That's the one."

"I think it speaks for itself."

"Oh. Then I won't disturb you further. Bye-bye."

"Bye-bye." The woman left and Carrie rejoined Stone. "That was close," she said.

"I should have stood up and greeted her," Stone said. "That's what she deserved."

Carrie laughed. "The sight of you naked is more than she deserved." They made love again, then they walked out to the pool and had a swim, joined by Bob, who liked chasing a ball around the pool.

They were lying on chaises later when the phone rang, and Carrie picked it up. "Hello? . . . Yes, he is." She handed Stone the phone. "It's your policeman."

Stone took the phone. "Hello?"

"Afternoon. Sorry to disturb you on a Sunday, but I have some news."

"Shoot."

"Darla Henry was a high-class prostitute out of Palm Beach. She's had two arrests in the past five years. Makes you wonder who she was selling her services to, doesn't it?"

"I have some news, too," Stone said. "James Carlton has hired me to represent him."

"Uh-oh."

"Don't think that way. He's flying in from London tomorrow afternoon, and he'd be happy to meet with you."

"When?"

"Say, six o'clock at his house?"

"Fine with me."

"Other news — he gave a party last New Year's Eve, before leaving for London the following day, and he can supply you with a

68

guest list."

"I'd really like to have a look at that."

"You will. He wants to have the house cleaned before his arrival. Are you finished with the room that was furnished with a corpse?"

"I guess so, we've been over it every which way twice. I don't think he'll want the mattress back."

"I don't think so, either. His stay will be short, so you probably won't get a second shot at him. You should plan accordingly."

"I'll do that, and I don't think it will take long."

"I'll let him know. See you tomorrow at six." He hung up. "Looks like you'll have me as a guest until Tuesday morning," he said to Carrie.

"I can stand that," she replied. "I just hope you're up to it."

"I'll steel myself," he said.

"Steel is good."

11

A little after four the following afternoon, Stone's cell phone rang. "Hello?"

"It's Jim Carlton. We're ten minutes out, so I'll see you at the house at five-thirty?"

"That's fine. Sergeant D'Orio will visit at six, and he's given the okay to clean the affected room, but you won't get the mattress back."

"He's welcome to it. See you soon."

Stone walked over to the Carlton house at five-thirty. The front door was open. "Hello?"

"Come in!" a male voice shouted. "In the study!"

Stone found a book-lined room off the living room, and Carlton rose from his desk to greet him. "Welcome," he said. "Can I get you a drink?"

"Business first," Stone said, taking a seat.

"The cleaners have gone, and that guest room smells like limes," he said, sinking back into his chair. "Do we know any more than the last time we spoke?"

"The police did a background check on Darla Henry," Stone replied. "She's a high-end pro, working out of Palm Beach."

"I can usually pick those out in a crowd," he said, "but nothing comes back to me from New Year's Eve." He handed Stone a sheet of paper. "Here's the party list."

Stone ran a quick eye down it, spotting some celebrity names, then his eye stopped. "Harvey Biggers?" he said.

"Yeah, he was there."

"It says, 'Harvey Biggers and guest.' Who was that, his wife?"

"No, they split. I chose sides. I remember a pretty girl, a blonde, with Harvey, but not her name."

Stone took a copy of the deceased's driver's license photo from his pocket and showed it to Carlton.

"That's the girl with Harvey," he said.

"Was Harvey staying overnight?"

"Nobody was booked in for the night, but some of them didn't want to drive and left the following morning, I guess. I left around eight AM, myself, and nobody was stirring. I gave instructions to the staff to give breakfast to anybody who turned up."

"Did you actually see Harvey that morning?"

"Nope. I don't even know if he stayed."

"Well, we know he didn't take his date with him."

"That's clear."

"Did you fly private?"

"Yep. I have a Gulfstream 450."

"That's a good way to travel."

"Do you have a Gulfstream?"

"No, but I often travel on them, courtesy of a business associate. I fly a Citation CJ3 Plus."

"Fly it yourself?"

"Yes."

"I have my private and my instrument and multiengine ratings. I'm scheduled for jet training Flight Safety in Wichita next month."

"You'll enjoy the town most from your hotel room, but that's okay, because you'll be too tired every night to go out."

Carlton laughed. "I've heard that. Do we need to talk any more about the body in the bedroom before the cops get here?"

"No, just tell him what you told me."

A voice came from the front door. "Hello?"

"I'll get him." Stone walked to the door. "In here, Sergeant."

D'Orio joined them, along with another man dressed in a suit. "This is my chief, Don Ferris."

Everybody shook hands and sat down. Carlton handed D'Orio his party guest list.

D'Orio took Carlton through his list of questions, then turned to Ferris. "You got anything, Chief?"

The chief handed D'Orio a sheet of paper, and D'Orio handed it to Carlton. "Do you recognize that photograph?"

"I do. She was with a guest of mine named Harvey Biggers. Apparently they stayed overnight, but as I said, I left for London before anybody was up."

"You have an address for Mr. Biggers?"

"It's on the guest list I gave you."

"Right. I think we'll want to have a word with Mr. Biggers."

"Was there any drug use at your party?" the chief asked.

"Not to my knowledge. I would have asked anyone using drugs to leave, but I don't know what they did in the bathrooms and guest rooms."

"Did you use any drugs yourself?"

"No, the only nonprescription drug I use is alcohol, and that lightly."

"Were you drunk that evening?"

"I don't get drunk."

"Were any of your guests drunk?"

"It was a New Year's Eve party, I imagine so. Some of them didn't want to drive and stayed here, but I didn't count heads. I went to bed around one AM, and the party was dying by then."

"Did you hear from Mr. Biggers at any time after the party?"

"No, but then I've been out of the country."

"Does your cell phone work out of the country?"

"Yes, but very few people have that number, and Harvey isn't one of them. I use a second cell phone for business, and only my staff have that number."

"Are you planning to leave town anytime soon, Mr. Carlton?"

"Yes, I'm leaving tomorrow for Los Angeles. I have a film to finish."

"Can you postpone your departure for a few days?" the chief asked.

Stone spoke for the first time. "Chief, Mr. Carlton is on a deadline to complete his film."

"We're opening on three thousand screens in six weeks," Carlton said, "and we haven't finished editing yet. We also have music and dubbing to do, and I may have to reshoot a scene or two. It's very tight."

"Mr. Carlton will make himself available to speak to you anytime you wish," Stone said. "He wants only to cooperate, within the constraints of his work."

"There'll be an opening at Radio City Music Hall," Carlton said, "for six thousand of my closest friends. I'll send you some tickets, if you like."

Both policemen nodded. "The wife would like that," the chief said.

The cops shook hands and left.

"The tickets were a nice touch," Stone said. "Cops never get invited anywhere."

"I figured," Carlton said. He handed Stone a card. "Send me your bill."

"Don't worry about it," Stone said, getting to his feet.

He handed Carlton his card.

"I'll send you some opening tickets, too, and better seats than the cops. And you're invited to the opening-night party at the Rainbow Room after the screening."

"Sounds good," Stone said. "If you should hear from Harvey Biggers, will you let me know?"

"You want his address?"

"I have it," Stone said. They shook hands, and Stone walked next door and surrendered himself to the tender mercies of Carrie Fiske, for one more night.

After they had made love, and just before Stone fell asleep, Carrie whispered in his ear, "I have an early appointment in the city tomorrow, so I'll be leaving here at four AM. Rupert will give you breakfast."

"Hmmmf," Stone replied, then drifted off.

12

Stone eased into consciousness at a little after ten o'clock. He was unaccustomed to sleeping that late, but at least, he thought, he'd miss the rush-hour traffic into Manhattan. He showered, shaved, dressed, and packed his bag, then carried it downstairs with him.

Rupert was ready for him and served a big breakfast, which he wolfed down. He'd skip lunch to make up for it. While he was on coffee, Rupert took his luggage out to the car, and he heard the trunk lid slam. Rupert came back shortly. "Everything's in your car," he said, "including a small gift from Ms. Fiske."

"Then I'll be on my way," Stone said.

"I'll be on my way, too," Rupert replied. "I've been given a week off." The two walked down to the front of the house together, and Rupert drove away. Stone followed until he lost the man at an intersection.

Stone lazily followed the GPS instructions to the Long Island Expressway, and as he entered the highway, someone kissed him on his right ear. He looked in the rearview mirror and found two large black eyes looking back at him.

"Bob, what the hell are you doing here?" he demanded, but he didn't get an answer. Bob hopped into the seat beside him and sat down. There was an envelope tied to his collar with Stone's name on it. He pulled into a rest stop and read it.

My Dear Stone,
You were the perfect guest, and the perfect lay, too. Thank you for a memorable time. I hope you'll come back soon and even before that. Call me in the city.

It's clear to me that you and Bob were made for each other. You're the first person he's ever shown much of an interest in, including me. His food, his vet records, and registration are all in his bag in your trunk, and you'll be glad to know that the documents making him legal to visit Britain are there, too. He's had all the right shots, etc. You'll find him easy to deal with. I'm leaving town for a couple of weeks this midday. If, when I get back, you and Bob turn out to have been incompatible, I'll take him off your hands, but I don't see that happening. Oh, and his meal schedule and some plastic bags are in his bag, too.

Kisses,
Carrie

"Well, Bob," Stone said to the dog, "it looks as if you and I are bunking together for a couple of weeks."

Bob's tail beat affirmatively against the leather seat.

He made good time to the house and pulled into the garage. He got out his and Bob's luggage, put his on the elevator and took Bob's with him to his office. Joan heard him close the outer door and came in to greet him.

"Well, who's this?" she cried, and knelt to greet the dog.

"This is Bob, and he's going to be spending a couple of weeks with us." He handed her the bag. "Here's his luggage, and there are all sorts of goodies in there. As I recall he has lunch around this time, and there's food in there, too."

Joan took the bag and came back with two bowls and set them on the floor next to

Stone's desk. "There you go, Bob. How about you, boss? Lunch?"

"I had an enormous breakfast, so I'll skip that."

"A good weekend?"

"Very good, and I got some new business." He handed her Carrie's will and gave her instructions on what to do with it. "A man called Nicky Chalmers will be calling to set up an appointment."

"He called this morning. Shall I get him back for you?"

"Sure. I also picked up a movie director called James Carlton, but I think that was a one-shot meeting." He sat down while Joan made the call.

"Nicky on one," she said.

Stone picked up the phone. "Good afternoon, Nicky."

"And to you, Stone."

"I just got back a moment ago, and somewhat to my surprise, Bob came with me. He's staying here while Carrie is out of town."

"We were all astonished at how Bob took to you. He's ordinarily pretty diffident, except at mealtime."

"Aren't we all?"

"Probably so. Can we get together tomorrow? I'd like to bring my business manager with me. His name is Duncan Beard."

"Shall I ask Bill Eggers to join us?"

"Sure, that would be nice, I haven't seen him in years."

"How about lunch here, then? Twelve-thirty? I'll round up Bill, if he's available."

"I'll look forward to it."

"You've got the address. Use the ground-floor street entrance."

"See you then."

Stone hung up and called Eggers. "You free for lunch here tomorrow? I've got a new client for you, name of Nicky Chalmers."

"Ah, the great-grandson of the Tire King, now a dilettante art collector of some note. Knew him at Yale. Delighted to have him, and I'll join you for lunch."

"Twelve-thirty. See you then. Come to the office." He buzzed Joan: "Tell Helene we'll be four for lunch tomorrow, serve something manly. We'll sit down at one."

"Got it. I'd better take Bob out, it's on his schedule."

"You two enjoy yourselves."

Around five Stone was cleaning up his desktop, in preparation for a drink and the TV news, when Bob came and sat next to him. "What's up, Bob?"

Bob didn't move, just fixed his gaze on Stone.

81

"Joan?"

She came in.

"Why is Bob staring at me?"

"Ah, his schedule says he dines at five. I'll serve him."

Bob got down his dinner, then returned to sit next to Stone and stare. "Joan?"

She came back. "I forgot, he gets a cookie after his meals and his trips outside." She handed Stone the biscuit, and he handed it to Bob, who then curled up beside Stone's desk and went to sleep.

Late that evening, as Stone was getting into his nightshirt, Bob came and sat down in front of him and gave him the staring treatment.

"What is it, Bob?"

Bob made a little noise, then went to the door.

"Ah, you want to go out?"

Bob wagged all over.

Five minutes later, Stone found himself walking around the block in his trench coat and slippers in the pouring rain, waiting for Bob to find just the right spot. This process took fifteen minutes. Back inside, Stone had to find a towel and rub Bob dry, or at least, drier. Bob then insisted on his cookie.

Stone turned on the late-evening news

and caught up on the day. Bob curled up in his bed and went straight to sleep.

"Not a care in the world," Stone muttered.

13

Stone had a good lunch with Nicky Chalmers, his business manager, and Bill Eggers, and all were agreed that Nicky would join Woodman & Weld as Stone's client. He saw them off after lunch, then went down to his office to find Sergeant D'Orio, in a civilian suit, waiting for him.

"Good afternoon, Sergeant."

"Good afternoon, Mr. Barrington."

"Would you like some coffee?"

"Your secretary gave me some, thanks."

"Then what else can we do for you?"

"I finally caught up with Harvey Biggers at his apartment."

"Good. And what did he have to say?"

"He said he picked up Darla Henry at a place called Bobby Van's."

"When?"

"On New Year's Eve. He said he didn't have a date for the party, so he invited her along. They got drunk, and late in the

84

evening, had sex. He slept for a while, then decided to leave, but he couldn't wake her up, so he just left her there."

"So they weren't old friends?"

"He denies ever having met her before that night."

"Have you any reason to doubt his word?"

"I've got no evidence that he's lying, it's just a feeling."

"I know that feeling. Biggers came to see me last week, claiming that his ex-wife, who is my client, was trying to kill him."

"And what did you do about that?"

"I showed him the door."

"Did he have two black eyes at the time?"

"Yes, he did." Stone told him the whole story.

"He's not quite over them, yet. There's something else. I didn't mention it before, but we found Darla's cell phone in her purse. We've had time to get the records, and I was surprised to see that she called you three times." He handed Stone the record sheet. "I thought you said you didn't know her."

"I didn't, and I don't." He ran a finger down the list and found the calls. "The calls are all to this office, and at a time when I was in England." He buzzed Joan, and she came in. "Did we receive three calls from a

Darla Henry on these dates?" He handed her the sheet.

"Now that you mention it, you had two or three calls from a woman who wouldn't give her name and hung up. You can see that none of these three lasted more than half a minute." She handed the sheet back, and Stone handed it back to D'Orio.

"There you go," he said. "I never spoke to her, and she didn't leave her name."

D'Orio sighed. "Every time I think I have something in this case, it just melts away."

"Would it help if I confessed to her murder?"

D'Orio's eyebrows shot up. "Yes, sir!"

"Sorry, I was just trying to make you feel better. I'm completely innocent, and so, I suspect, is Harvey Biggers."

"Why do you think so?"

"Just a gut feeling. Also, his story makes perfect sense, and I'll bet the bartender at Bobby Van's will back him up."

"It was a long time ago," the cop said.

"Jim Carlton remembered her from the same night, and he'd never seen her before. She must have been a memorable lady."

"You have a point. I'll stop by Bobby Van's on the way home."

"If you hurry, you'll miss the worst of the rush-hour traffic."

"Right." D'Orio stood up.

Stone walked him to the outside door. "Listen, I used to be a cop, and sometimes you get ahold of a bad situation that turns out not to be a crime. I think it's highly probable that Harvey and Darla met at Bobby Van's, he took her to the party, succumbed to her charms, then left, and Darla, who was probably drunk, died of a mixture of sleeping pills and alcohol. And I'll bet, when your tox screen comes back, that's what it'll say."

"I have a feeling you're right," D'Orio said. "Thanks for your time."

They shook hands, and he went on his way.

Joan had gotten into her coat and had Bob on his leash. "Turns out Bob's annual physical is due. I'm taking him uptown to see his personal physician and get his rabies inoculation updated, et cetera, et cetera. Fred will man the phones while I'm gone."

"Okay, see you later." He looked into her office and found Fred at her desk.

"Nice dog, Bob," Fred said. "I had one like him as a boy."

"I never had a dog as a boy. My mother was allergic."

"Good thing you're not, then."

"I guess it is a good thing."

"Want to make a small wager?"

"On what?"

"I'll bet you twenty quid — ah, bucks — that when the lady comes home, she won't get her dog back."

"You're on," Stone said, "and I'll enjoy taking your money."

14

Stone was back at his desk when Dino called. "I hear you were caught in bed with a dead woman in the Hamptons."

"You have big ears, but faulty hearing. I *reported* a dead woman, and she was in no condition to go to bed with. Who have you been talking to?"

"Their chief out there, Don Ferris. Known him for years."

"Did he tell you what his latest theory is? He has lots of them."

"His latest theory is you."

"Well, his sergeant just left here, after being straightened out on that point. I'm no longer a suspect, if I ever was."

"What's *your* theory?"

"A guy named Harvey Biggers —"

"That's a name? Sounds like somebody out of *Country Gentleman* magazine, circa 1950."

"It does, doesn't it? You want to hear this,

or you want to talk?"

"Go."

"Harvey Biggers meets her at the bar at Bobby Van's and invites her to Jim Carlton's New Year's Eve party. They get drunk and hit the sack. The girl takes a few Ambien. Biggers decamps at dawn, says he can't wake her. Carlton goes to London for three months, and I discover the body, which is three months old."

"Sounds like fun."

"Do you remember what that smells like?"

"All too well."

"We were having a very nice lobster salad at lunch next door when the wind shifted and ruined our appetites. I took a look around and called nine-one-one. The rest is everybody just certifying the obvious."

"You want to have dinner tonight? Seven-thirty at Patroon?"

"Sure. Can I bring my new roommate, Bob? It would hurt his feelings if I didn't ask him."

"You have a new roommate, and she's named *Bob*?"

"He."

Dino was uncharacteristically silent.

"See you at seven-thirty. Bob is looking forward to meeting you." Stone hung up, laughing.

Stone and Bob arrived at Patroon on time and were greeted by the owner, Ken Aretzky. Bob offered him a paw.

"You are pet-friendly, aren't you, Ken?" Stone asked.

"I don't know," Ken said, shaking the paw, "it never came up." Ken showed him to a booth, and seated Bob under the table. Stone ordered a drink.

"Anything for Bob?"

"He's on the wagon — he made a fool of himself last time."

Stone's drink arrived, followed shortly by Dino and his wife, Vivian. "Okay, where's this Bob?"

"Under the table — he never could hold his liquor."

Dino jumped. "He still can't, he just licked my hand."

Viv peeked under the tablecloth. "Hello, Bob," she said. "He licked my hand, too."

"It's the friendly thing to do."

"How did you and Bob come to meet?" Dino asked.

"We met in the Hamptons last weekend, and he hitched a ride to the city with me."

"You were never the dog type."

91

"That's because I was denied that pleasure as a child. My mother was allergic, or at least said she was."

"That's a good excuse for not letting you have a dog," Viv said.

"That's what I suspected. Anyway, my custody is only temporary. Bob is going back to his mom in a couple of weeks."

"Awwww," Viv said. "And he's so nice."

A waiter appeared with a T-bone on a silver platter, and Bob accepted it with alacrity.

"I'll bet that's the first time anybody has ever been served a bone in this joint," Dino said.

"No doubt." Dino's and Viv's drinks arrived.

"Dino tells me you were caught with a dead woman last weekend," Viv said.

"I'll bet he did," Stone replied. "He's having a good time with that one."

"Tell me the whole story."

Stone gave her a rapid-fire account.

"You lead such an interesting life," Viv said.

"I do, don't I?"

"Glad you're not married to him?" Dino asked.

"Fairly glad. You lead an interesting life, too."

"I ran a check on this Harvey Biggers," Dino said.

"And?"

"He got busted on a domestic disturbance last year."

"With Carrie Fiske?"

"That was the name."

"Is it policy to always arrest the husband in these things?"

"Not exactly, but if the wife makes the call, it often works out that way."

"Did either of them have any marks or bruises?"

"I didn't read that far."

"Anything else on the Biggers sheet?"

"Yeah, the year before last he called nine-one-one from a motel in West Palm Beach — a woman in his bed, unresponsive."

15

Stone stared at Dino. "Oh, shit."

"My reaction exactly," Dino said.

"Why didn't the East Hampton cops come up with that?"

"Beats me — maybe they searched the wrong databases."

"Hang on." Stone got out his cell phone and called Carrie Fiske. The call went directly to voice mail. "Hello, Carrie, this is Stone. I've just gotten some new information about Harvey. I don't know where you are, but it's imperative that you stay as far away from him as possible. If he turns up, call the police and accuse him of stalking you. Call me back at your earliest opportunity." He hung up. "I'm back."

"Your client?" Dino asked.

"My client's voice mail."

"Where is she?"

"Out of town. I don't know where."

"Where is Harvey Biggers?"

"He must be in New York. Sergeant D'Orio said he talked to him today. I'd better call the East Hampton cops. What is that chief's name again?"

"I've already called him," Dino said. "Got him before he left the city, so they're either talking to him right now or looking for him."

"Biggers came to see me, you know."

"But you're representing his wife."

"I put Fred on bodyguard duty with Carrie Fiske. Biggers showed up and tried to get at her, ignoring Fred. Fred broke his nose, and a couple of cops sent him to the hospital. He was packing, too, according to Fred, but he didn't get busted for that. He must have a permit."

Dino got out his cell phone and made a call, then hung up. "He does. I just canceled it, so if he gets picked up again, they'll hold him. Why did he come to see you?"

"To convince me that *he* was about to be killed by Carrie."

"That's weird."

"Yeah, he almost convinced me. Now I have lingering doubts to dismiss."

They ordered dinner, then Stone tried again to reach Carrie, with the same result.

"You're looking worried," Viv said.

"That's because I don't know where she

is, and I don't know where Harvey is, either."

"I'll call Ferris," Dino said. He listened, left a message, and hung up. "He'll call when he gets the message."

"Well," Viv said, "at least we know she's not in New York, where Harvey was last sighted."

"No, we don't know that. She may have told me that to keep me from returning Bob."

"Why would you want to return Bob? He's lovely!"

"This was sort of a practical joke. She left for the city and left Bob in my car with a note, saying she'd be away for a couple of weeks."

"And how does Bob feel about that?"

"Perfectly fine, as far as I know. You can ask him, he's under the table."

Viv lifted the tablecloth and checked. "He's occupied with a T-bone and doesn't wish to be disturbed."

Dinner came and they ate, but everybody was preoccupied now.

Dino's phone rang. "Bacchetti. Yeah, Don. Have you got eyes on Harvey Biggers? Well, I dug back a couple of years and found that he called nine-one-one in West Palm and reported an unresponsive woman in his bed, who was DOA. Yeah, I thought that was interesting, too. I'm with Stone Barrington, and Biggers's ex-wife is his client. He's worried about her, and he can't find her. Is that enough for you to take Biggers back to East Hampton for a while? I see. Will you add carrying a concealed weapon without a permit to the charges? That should be enough to pick him up. No, he *had* a permit — I canceled it. Keep me posted, will you? And let me know if you need assistance from my people." Dino hung up. "They last saw him at home, so they'll knock on his door again."

"I'd really like to have him off the street," Stone said.

"Is East Hampton far enough away? That's where they'll take him for questioning, if he's still there."

"That'll do for the time being."

Dino's phone went off. "Bacchetti. Yeah, Don. We'll handle it. Give me an address. Ten minutes, tops." He broke off the call and pressed a speed dial number. "This is Bacchetti. I want a man picked up, one Harvey Biggers." He gave the address. "Hold him on a charge of carrying a concealed weapon without a permit. He had one, I canceled it. Get back to me." He hung up.

"Biggers didn't answer his door, but he should be in the bag shortly, then you can relax and have dessert."

They had dessert, then Dino's phone rang again. "Bacchetti. Well, shit. Issue an APB on my authority, and call me when he's in cuffs." He hung up. "He wasn't at home."

They had coffee then broke up. Stone walked Bob home for the exercise. Fortunately, he had brought plastic bags.

Stone was unlocking his front door when he heard a shoe scuff on the steps behind him. "Good evening, Mr. Barrington," a deep voice said.

Stone turned to find Harvey Biggers standing there, holding a pistol.

16

Stone stared at the gun barrel: a 45. He wasn't going to argue with that. "Of course," he said, opening the door. "Come right in." Bob ran ahead; Stone dropped the leash, slammed the door behind him, and stepped out of the line of fire. He heard muffled swearing from outside, and there was banging on the door.

Stone called Dino.

"Bacchetti."

"It's Stone. Biggers is on my front steps with a .45, banging on my door."

"Hang on." Dino went off-line, then came back seconds later. "There's a car four blocks from you. It's on the way."

"Thank you for that."

"Can you keep him occupied until it arrives?"

"I'll see." Stone picked up the intercom next to the door and pressed a button. "Mr. Biggers? Are you there?"

"You son of a bitch, you invited me in!"

"You might recall that I was under duress at the time."

"Duress? I didn't threaten you."

"Mr. Biggers, you pointed a gun at me."

"Well, I've never shot anybody before."

"Gee, I wish you'd told me, I'd have let you right in." Stone heard a police siren; sounded like a couple of blocks away. He heard footsteps on the intercom. "Mr. Biggers?" He went back to his cell phone. "Your cops used their siren, scared him off."

"They wouldn't have done that — I told them to keep it quiet. It was probably another car answering a different call."

"That's comforting."

"Well, at least he's carrying. We've got a legit beef to take him in."

"Let me know if that gets done, will you? I'll have to take Bob out in the morning, and I'd like to know that I won't get shot while Bob is pooping."

"Yeah, sure. Go to bed." Dino hung up, and Stone and Bob went upstairs. Bob seemed to like the elevator.

Stone turned over and flung out an arm, and he was greeted with a grunt. He opened an eye. "Bob? Nobody invited you onto my bed."

Bob opened an eye, regarded him coolly, then rolled over and went back to sleep.

Stone was about to get up and throw Bob at his own bed when the phone rang. He glanced at the bedside clock: 6:05 AM.

He picked up the phone. "What?" he muttered.

"Good morning. It's Carrie."

"It's six o'clock in the morning, what's good about that?"

"Oh, I'm sorry, it's the time difference. I got it wrong."

"Where are you?"

"Out of town."

"It's important that you stay there, until the coast is clear."

"Clear of what?"

"Not what, who. Rather, whom?"

"Is it Harvey?"

"He greeted me on my front steps when I came home last night and pointed a gun at me."

"That thing? It's never loaded."

"I didn't feel I could count on that."

"He wouldn't hurt a . . ."

"Ex-wife?"

"Well . . ."

"Carrie, twice in the past two years Harvey has been reported with a female corpse in his bed. Does that give you any ideas?"

"Was one of them next door to my East Hampton house?"

"Yes."

"Where was the other?"

"West Palm."

"Oh."

"Carrie, one female corpse in a fellow's bed can be explained away, maybe — two, not so easy. Unless you want to try for the number three slot, stay out of New York, East Hampton, or any other place that Harvey might think to find you."

"You're serious?"

"Carrie, when you came to me because you were afraid of your ex-husband, were you serious?"

"Yes, I suppose I was, but I was upset."

"And that was before you knew about the two corpses."

"You have a point."

"I have more than a point, Carrie, I have a serious concern for your safety, and so should you. The police are looking for Harvey as we speak, and I've no doubt they'll bag him soon."

"Has Harvey actually done anything?"

"He's carrying an unlicensed firearm."

"But he told me he has a license."

"Not anymore. I arranged for it to be canceled, so the police would have cause to detain him."

"Weren't two lady corpses enough?"

"Not until enough evidence has been found to prove he caused their deaths."

"What kind of evidence?"

"Say, a bullet in one of their brains that matches his gun — like that."

"Was either of them shot?"

"So far, the causes of death are undetermined."

"So, what other kind of evidence?"

"Forensic evidence."

"You mean, like on TV?"

"Exactly like that — fibers, hairs, blood, DNA, fingerprints. Also, the old-fashioned kind of evidence — motive, means, and opportunity."

"How are you and Bob getting along?"

"Don't change the subject."

"But I'm concerned about Bob."

"When you've convinced me that you're taking this threat seriously, we can talk about Bob."

"All right, I'm taking it seriously. I won't come home until you say I can."

"Good. Now how can I get ahold of you?"

She gave him a number. "That's my cell. It works everywhere."

"That's good enough."

"Now, how about you and Bob?"

"We're both fine."

"Are you enjoying each other's company?"

"I can only speak for myself — Bob has been quiet on the subject."

"Has he bitten you or growled at you?"

"Neither. He's been a perfect gentleman. I took him out to dinner last night, and he behaved beautifully."

"Where?"

"Patroon."

"Isn't that a steak house?"

"Steaks are on the menu."

"That was dangerous, Bob likes his beef."

"He got a large bone and was perfectly content."

"I've got to run, baby. You two take care of each other."

Before Stone could reply, she had hung up.

Bob edged across the bed and rested his head on Stone's stomach.

"It was for you," Stone said. "Your mama is fine."

17

Stone fed Bob, then led him to the elevator, stood him up on his hind legs and held his paw to the elevator button. "Remember this," he said. The door opened, and Bob walked on. Stone put his finger on the office-level button. "Remember this, too, it's a two-step process." He pressed the button and the elevator and Bob went down.

Stone got his breakfast from the dumbwaiter, set it on the bed, and got back in. His phone rang. "Yes?"

"It's Joan. I was standing in your office when Bob got off the elevator alone. How'd he do that?"

"I explained it to him."

"Oh."

"Bob's had his breakfast and wants to go out. May I eat mine now? You won't have to take me out."

"Enjoy." Joan hung up.

Later, Stone was at his desk when Joan

buzzed. "Dino on one."

He pressed the button. "Good morning."

"Yeah, you too. My guys found your pal Biggers, two blocks from your house. He said he'd just gotten off a Second Avenue bus."

"And they bought that?"

"No, they searched him and found no gun."

"So, he ditched it."

"Probably. He was wearing a .45 holster on his belt."

"Aha!"

"No aha. They couldn't arrest him for carrying a concealed holster."

"Why not? I should think that would be prima facie evidence of carrying a gun."

"He said he had worn the same pants for two days and forgot that the holster was on his belt."

"So he confessed to having a gun on him the day before."

"Yeah, but he said he wasn't in the city then."

"Yeah, but you have a witness who saw him carrying a gun."

"Who, you?"

"Yeah, me."

"You know as well as I do that eyewitness testimony is often wrong."

"Not when *I'm* the eyewitness."

"You have a high opinion of your own perspicacity."

"I know a .45 caliber Glock when I see it — that's perspicacious enough."

"Not in a court of law. A good defense attorney would call your perspicaciousness into question. He'd say you *wanted* to see a .45 Glock in the man's hand, therefore you *thought* you saw it."

"My perspifuckingcaciousness is just fine, thank you. I remind you that I'm a veteran police officer."

"You *were* a veteran police officer. The clock goes back to zero when you retire."

"Well, then, I'm a veteran *former* police officer."

"I don't have time to mince words with you, I have thirty-six thousand, six hundred police officers to command."

"Mince *this*!" Stone shouted into the phone, but it was too late; Dino had already hung up.

Joan was standing in the doorway, leaning against the jamb. "You seem a little on edge," she said.

"I'm just fine."

"No, you're steaming — even Bob noticed." She nodded toward the dog, who was sitting next to Stone's desk, staring anxiously at him.

"Bob, I'm just fine," he said.

"Bob's not buying it," Joan said. "Why don't you get out of town for a while, until they pick up this guy."

"Where would you like me to go?"

"Pick something from your extensive list of real estate holdings," she said, "and go."

"I just got back," Stone pointed out.

"That's no excuse."

"You're just trying to get rid of me."

"Nope, Harvey Biggers is trying to get rid of you."

"He's not smart enough to get rid of me."

"He doesn't have to be smart, he just has to be lucky."

"Arguing with you is like arguing with Dino."

She brightened. "Thank you very much."

"It wasn't meant as a compliment."

"I knew that, but I liked it anyway."

Stone leaned on his elbows and put his face in his hands. Bob walked over and rested his chin on Stone's knee, slowly wagging his tail.

"Bob and I think you should get out of town," Joan said. The phone rang, and she picked up the one on Stone's desk. "The Barrington Practice," she said, "or Woodman & Weld, take your pick."

108

Stone made a groaning noise.

"Well, hi there, how are you?" Joan said, brightening. "He's right here." She handed Stone the phone. "It's Ed Eagle, calling from Santa Fe."

"You're just saying that to cheer me up," Stone said, taking the phone from her.

18

Stone was genuinely glad to hear from Ed Eagle. "Ed, how are you?"

"Better than middling, I guess. How about you?"

"Not too bad."

"You very busy these days?"

"No, I spent some time in England and just got back a couple of weeks ago."

"I have an invitation for you."

"I accept."

"Hang on, let me finish. Susannah is having a birthday, and I'm throwing a party for her."

"I accept."

"It's in Santa Fe this weekend."

"I accept. Which birthday?"

"Don't ask. How soon can you get your ass out here?"

"Is tomorrow too soon?"

"Certainly not. What are you flying these days?"

"A Citation CJ3 Plus."

"Then you can do it nonstop?"

"As long as there isn't a two-hundred-knot headwind."

"See you late tomorrow afternoon, then?"

"Perfect."

"Don't rent a car, I'll loan you one. It'll be at the airport."

"Great."

"And there's something I want to show you."

"What's that?"

"You'll see."

"By the way, I have a houseguest named Bob. May I bring him along?"

"Sure, as long as you don't mind sleeping in the same bed. We've got a full house."

"No problem, Bob can sleep on the floor."

"Stone, is there something you want to tell me?"

"Lots of things, but not now."

"By the way, when you get to the airport, read the instructions in the manual before you start the car."

"I know how to start a car, Ed."

"Trust me — read the instructions."

"Whatever you say."

"Can you find your way to the house sober?"

"I can."

"Then we'll see you tomorrow. Drinks are at six."

"I'll flight-plan for the cocktail hour."

"See you then."

"See you." Stone hung up feeling elated.

"You look better already," Joan said.

"I feel better already."

"Bob looks relieved," she said.

"Are you relieved, Bob?"

Bob wagged all over.

"You want me to pack you a bag?"

"That would be great."

"How long?"

"Say a week, to be safe, and pack Bob a bag, too."

The following morning at ten, Stone sat at the end of runway 24 at Teterboro Airport.

"November One, Two, Three, Tango Foxtrot, cleared for take-off," the tower controller said.

"N123TF, cleared for takeoff."

Stone flipped on the pitot heat, strobes, and landing light, taxied onto the runway, and pushed the throttles forward, glancing at the pilot's display as the airspeed climbed. At a speed labeled R for rotate, Stone pulled back on the yoke, and the jet rose from the concrete and climbed. He retracted the landing gear and the flaps and, at 450 feet, switched on the autopilot, which would now fly the departure procedure known as RUDY4.

Shortly, he got a vector and a new altitude from the departure controller and, to his surprise, was given flight level 400, or 40,000 feet, and was cleared direct SAF.

Twenty minutes later he was at altitude and on course. He adjusted the air-conditioning, chose the symphony channel on the Sirius Satellite Radio, and picked up the *New York Times* crossword puzzle. He glanced over a shoulder to see how his new crew was doing and saw Bob sitting on a rear seat, looking intently out the window. Stone had laid a blanket in the aisle for him, and a moment later Bob hopped down, curled up, and went to sleep.

Stone concentrated on the puzzle. Each time he moved to the next clue, he looked up, did an instrument scan, made an adjustment, if necessary, then returned to the puzzle. Three and a half hours later he was descending into Santa Fe, with fifty minutes of fuel left, and he set down smoothly on runway 20.

As he taxied to a halt at the FBO (fixed-base operator) and stopped for chocking, a sleek dark sports car pulled up to the nose of the airplane. He wasn't sure what it was.

He picked up the checklist and went through the shutdown procedure, then got up and opened the door. Bob preceded him onto the ramp, and he gave the key to a lineman, who opened the forward baggage compartment and loaded his and Bob's luggage into the rear of the car. It was a tight fit.

Stone walked around the car and found the Aston Martin winged logo. The lineman walked Bob over to some grass to do some business while Stone sat in the driver's seat and looked around. He couldn't find a key or a start button, and there was no gearshift lever present in the usual place.

"You know this car?" the lineman asked.

"I don't."

"I had to read up on it before I took it out of the hangar. Here's what you do. First, set the handbrake, since the gearbox has no Park setting. Put your foot on the brake, and put this into that slot on the panel." He handed Stone a little black box, and he slid it into the slot. "Now push it all the way in." Stone did so, and the car leapt to life with an attractive roar.

"Now you got two choices. You can shift up with the right paddle and down with the left paddle, or you can push the D button on the panel, which will give you an automatic transmission. You lift your foot a little to change gears, or let the car decide. When you stop, pull on both paddles for neutral, or push the N button, apply the handbrake, and push the key again." Stone tried that, and the key popped out.

"Got it," Stone said, and drove over to the electric gate. A moment later he was cruising away, with Bob in the passenger seat.

By the time he spotted the stone eagle on the road above the village of Tesuque, Stone felt at home in the car. He pulled into the drive and Ed Eagle, all six feet seven inches of him, walked out of the house to greet him.

19

Stone and Ed shook hands and hugged, while Bob helped Ed's man with the luggage. "Good flight?" Ed asked as they walked into the house.

"Perfect. The winds were easy on me." Stone looked ahead into the living room. "Uh-oh," he said. Bob was standing stock-still in the middle of the room, cautiously regarding a nearly identical Labrador retriever.

"That's Earl," Ed said. "Let them sort it out."

Some sniffing and circling took place, then Earl found a ball, showed it to Bob, and let it bounce from his mouth.

"They're fast friends now," Ed said. "Earl doesn't usually share his ball with visitors."

"Where's Susannah?" Stone asked.

"She's picking up someone at the airport."

"And what was it you wanted to show me?"

"All in good time."

Two other couples came into the room; one pair was Nicky and Vanessa Chalmers, the other he didn't know.

"I understand you and the Chalmerses have met," Ed said. "These other folks are Carlos and Candela Munoz, from San Antonio."

Everyone shook hands. "Nicky is my newest client," Stone said.

"And he's one of my oldest," Ed replied. "I defended his company against a lawsuit the first year I practiced, and we had a favorable outcome."

"Stone," Nicky said, "you didn't think I hired you without a reference, did you?"

"I'm glad you chose Ed for that," Stone replied.

Ed's man, Juan, came back into the room and took drink orders, and everybody took a seat while he served them. The two dogs rolled happily on the floor.

Stone heard a car door slam outside, and Susannah and a slightly younger and even more beautiful version of her came into the house. Susannah hugged Stone. "This is my little sister, Gala," she said. They shook hands, and she sat down next to Stone and ordered a drink. Stone could not take his eyes off Gala.

Ed passed by and whispered to Stone, "That's what I wanted to show you."

"Where do you hail from?" Stone asked Gala.

"Interesting question," she said. "I'm not sure. I've been living in Los Angeles the past few years, but I gave up the house there in a divorce. I got the Santa Fe house, and I've been redoing it, but I haven't decided yet if this is home."

"You could do worse," Stone said.

"I *have* done worse," she said, laughing. "I understand you live all over the place."

"I can't deny that, but I'm based in New York. I just keep getting offered houses I can't refuse. In my defense, I did sell one this year."

"You're a lawyer, I understand. How do you get any work done?"

"It's amazing how much work you can get done with a phone, a fax machine, and a computer. There seems to be less and less demand for face-to-face meetings, and even those can be done with the computer. What do you do?"

"I'm a screenwriter," she said.

"How many face-to-face meetings do you have a year?"

"Not many," she said. "I'm proof of your point, and my work is portable, so I can live

118

wherever I like." She nodded toward the two dogs. "Which one of those is yours?" she asked.

"Tell you the truth, I'm not sure. Oh, the one with the red collar is Bob, who flew out here with me. He's a good crew."

"What's a good crew?"

"One who doesn't complain about my flying."

"Bob doesn't look like the complaining sort," she said.

"Not so far."

"Have you known each other long?"

"Almost a week."

"So you didn't raise him from a pup?"

"No, I was visiting a client in East Hampton last weekend, and Bob seemed to prefer me to her. After I drove away, I found him in my backseat."

"I heard that," Nicky said. "I was there, and I can confirm it. Bob took to Stone immediately — the rest of us might have been chopped liver."

"Including the lady next door," Vanessa said.

"You don't want to know about that," Stone said to Gala. "Not before dinner anyway."

"I'll remind myself to ask after dinner," she said.

"At your own risk."

They talked for another half hour, then Juan called them to dinner. Stone found himself seated next to Gala, and he didn't argue about it.

Later in the evening they had coffee in Ed's study.

"Are you staying with the Eagles?" Stone asked Gala.

"No, I'm staying at my own place, in Tesuque village."

"Can I give you a lift home later?"

"That won't be necessary, I have my own car. You were kind enough to drive it from the airport for me."

"I didn't know," Stone said. "Why was it at the airport?"

"I was in L.A., so the dealer delivered it to the airport. I flew into Albuquerque, and Susannah picked me up."

"Where was it delivered from?"

"Broomfield, between Denver and Boulder. It's the closest dealer."

"You're going to love the car," Stone said.

"I'm sorry you can't drive me home," she said. "We'll have to think of another excuse to get you to my house."

"I don't need an excuse."

"Then why don't you come to lunch tomorrow?"

"I can't think of an excuse not to," he replied.

20

The following day Stone borrowed a Range Rover from Ed and drove into Tesuque. He found the house easily, just along from the village post office, and the gate was open so he drove in and parked in front of the house.

Gala met him at the door. "Come in," she said, leading him through a large living room with a fireplace at each end, then outside to where some comfortable furniture was arranged before a fireplace under a portico. "Bloody Marys are a specialty of the house," she said. "May we get you one?"

"Certainly. This will be my third Bloody Mary in a week," Stone said.

Gala gave the order to a motherly-looking Hispanic woman, who returned shortly with two tall glasses. "This is Maria, who has taken care of me for as long as I can remember."

"How do you do, Maria?"

"Very well, thank you." She returned to

the kitchen.

"You know," Stone said, "I've known Susannah for quite a while now, but she has certainly kept your existence a secret."

"We didn't see each other for several years. My ex-husband managed to alienate Susannah and Ed early in our marriage, something he was very good at, and he was persona non grata at their house. Out of misplaced loyalty, I stayed away, too."

"It's difficult for me to imagine someone who couldn't get along with Susannah and Ed — they're such pleasant people."

"Boris could evoke hostility in even the nicest people," Gala said.

"What was your married name?"

"Tirov — he was Russian. He made a name for himself there as an actor, and later a director, then came to this country in his early thirties."

"Did he do a series of some sort of superhero pictures?"

"Yes, he did, and in so doing simultaneously made a large fortune and gained a reputation as a hack, and an unpleasant one at that."

"How long were you married?"

"Nearly eight years. I suppose I was a glutton for punishment. He was subject to violent rages and brutish behavior, but only when we were alone. Among others he mustered some charm."

"I don't want you to relive all that on my account."

"Thank you, I'm doing a pretty good job of forgetting it."

"Then we won't need to talk of it again."

"What about you? Have you ever been married?"

"Yes, but more briefly than I would have liked. We'd been married for less than a year when she was murdered by a former lover."

"That's awful!"

"Yes, it was."

"I don't suppose there were children."

"One, a boy, conceived twenty-odd years ago. He's a film director in L.A."

"Oh, wait — Peter Barrington?"

"That's my boy."

"I love his work. I'd love to write something for him."

"He's pretty much an auteur," Stone said. "He and his partner, Ben Bacchetti, produce together."

"Ah, yes, the new CEO at Centurion Pictures."

"Ben's father is my closest friend. We were police detectives together in our youth. Dino is now the police commissioner of New York City."

"You seem very unlike a policeman."

"That's what the policemen I worked with thought. Dino was the only one I really got along with. First chance they got, they got rid of me, using an injury as an excuse. Best thing that ever happened to me."

"Then you went to law school?"

"I did that first, before the police academy. Afterward an old law school classmate urged me to take the bar exam, then join his firm. That worked out rather well."

"I seem to remember that your son is the stepson of the actor Vance Calder."

"That's correct. His mother left me for him before she knew she was pregnant."

"Did Calder know?"

"A good question. I think he may have suspected, but who knows? Neither he nor my former wife is around to answer that question."

"But Peter took your name?"

"That was his decision. I was very pleased when he told me."

"Do you see a lot of him?"

"Not enough. We spent some quality time together at my home in England this spring, while he was working on a film there. Both he and Ben married their girlfriends there, too, and it was nice to be around for that."

They had just finished lunch when a

distant telephone rang, and Maria appeared, a cordless instrument in her hand. "The phone is for Mr. Barrington," she said.

"That's odd. How would anybody know to reach me here?"

"Only one way to find out," Gala said.

Stone took the phone from her. "Hello?"

"Stone, it's Nicky Chalmers."

"Hello, Nicky."

"Vanessa and I are in town, having lunch with some friends, and I saw Carrie Fiske's ex-husband, Harvey Biggers, across the plaza, browsing the jewelry from the Indians who sell under the portico at the old governor's mansion. I mention this because Carrie said he's been stalking her, and you've been helping her deal with that."

"Did you speak to him?"

"No, it was just a fleeting glimpse."

"Nicky, if he turns up again you should avoid him. I'll explain why later."

"Avoiding Harvey will be a pleasure." Nicky hung up.

21

Stone stayed at Gala's house until almost three o'clock; then he got back into his borrowed Range Rover and, instead of returning to the Eagles' residence, turned toward Santa Fe and drove into the town.

He found a parking place half a block from the plaza, then he took a very slow walk around, checking every shop and every bench in the little park. He walked over to the old governor's mansion, one of the oldest buildings in the United States, parts of it dating back to the sixteenth century. A group of Native American jewelry makers were camped on the sidewalk, under the portico, selling their jewelry. Stone strolled along the sidewalk, looking less at the jewelry and more at the people. Harvey Biggers was not among them.

After an hour of searching the area, Stone got back into the Range Rover and drove back to Tesuque, through the village and up to the Eagle residence. There were caterers' trucks and a flower van parked out front, and inside, the living room was being decorated for Susannah's birthday party, and a man was tuning the grand piano.

Stone wandered into Ed's study and found Nicky Chalmers reading a book about Winchester rifles. Nicky looked up at him. "I'm sorry if I interrupted your lunch with my phone call," he said, "but I thought you'd want to know about Harvey."

Stone sat down on the sofa beside Nicky. "Do you have any idea why he's here?"

"None whatever," Nicky replied, "unless he's still stalking Carrie."

"Since I last saw you, Harvey has been connected to the corpse next door to Carrie Fiske's house in East Hampton. Not only that, he was found in similar circumstances in West Palm Beach two years ago."

"That's a very disturbing coincidence," Nicky said.

"It is indeed. And a couple of days ago, Harvey turned up on my doorstep with a gun."

"Jesus! I've known Harvey since Yale, and I wouldn't have suspected him of something like that. I guess he's just crazy over the divorce."

"That's my feeling. I managed to get into

the house and shut the door before he could think about using it."

"Do you think that was his intention?"

"I wish I knew the answer to that question. Let me ask you another, one that I suspect you're not supposed to tell me the answer to."

"And what would that be?"

"Where is Carrie?"

"Ah," Nicky said, "you're quite right, I took an oath not to tell you."

"Let me take a guess," Stone said. "Maybe you'll tell me if I'm wrong. Is Carrie in Santa Fe?"

"No," Nicky said without hesitation.

"Near Santa Fe?"

"Now I'm getting uncomfortable."

"How near?"

"An hour or two, perhaps. I'm not sure."

"Do you know how Carrie and I became acquainted?"

"She told me she went to see you about her will."

Stone sighed.

"Is that, strictly speaking, not true?" Nicky asked.

"Strictly speaking, no. The conversation eventually turned to that, and her will was, ostensibly, the reason I was in East Hampton when we met. Unfortunately, I'm sworn not to tell you the first reason we met."

"Ah, attorney-client confidentiality?"

"Yes."

"Perhaps I could have a guess?"

"If you like."

"Was Carrie concerned about her safety? Specifically, with regard to Harvey?"

Stone nodded. "I can neither confirm nor deny that."

Nicky smiled.

"You said, I believe, you knew Harvey at Yale?"

"Yes. We were on the rowing team together, and we were quite a good one. Harvey was an oar. I, given my smaller stature, was coxswain."

"May I ask, given your long acquaintance, what is your opinion of Harvey?"

"You may ask, but being of long acquaintance doesn't mean we saw a lot of each other after Yale. Not even at Yale, truth be told, except when afloat. Harvey was then, and at times since, ah . . . mercurial, shall we say."

"Mercurial to the point of being unstable?"

"I'm not sure I'm qualified, by training or constant exposure, to answer that in the affirmative. I can tell you, though, that at Yale, Harvey was quick to anger and quick to use his fists when angry. I've heard reports from others to suggest that that has not changed in the succeeding years."

"Do you know if he ever hurt anybody?"

"At Yale, he didn't lose any fights. Harvey was, then as now, tall and muscular. He may have run to fat a bit over the years, but who among us hasn't?"

Stone ignored that. "Nicky," Stone said, "do you suppose that tomorrow you and I might get into a car, take a drive, and accidentally bump into Carrie Fiske?"

"I've got a better idea," Nicky said, removing a cell phone from his pocket. "Why don't I just call her?"

Stone stood up. "I'll take a short walk," he said. "Tell her that Harvey is in Santa Fe, that I'm concerned for her safety, and that she can't have Bob back."

22

Nicky handed Stone the phone. "It's not a very good connection, I'm afraid."

Stone took the phone. "Hello?" He got a garbled voice. "Can you hear me, Carrie?" More garbling. "It's Stone. If you can hear me, call me on my cell when your signal improves." He hung up and gave the phone back to Nicky. "Where the hell is she, Nicky?"

"In Abiquiu." He spelled it. "It's up north from here, the landscape where Georgia O'Keeffe lived and painted. Carrie wanted to photograph the area."

"Does cell reception get any better than that?"

"I don't know, it's the first time I've tried."

"Will you go up there with me tomorrow morning?"

"Yes, if you like."

"Right after breakfast."

"Okay."

Juan came into the room and inquired as to whether he could get them anything.

"A glass of iced tea, please," Nicky replied.

"Make that two," Stone said.

When the tea came it was delicious, and Stone was thirsty.

"May I ask, what sort of relationship do you and Carrie have?"

"Nonprofessionally, quite cordial," Stone replied. "Professionally — well, she doesn't listen."

"Do you really think Harvey is a threat to her?"

"Nicky, do you really think Harvey is entirely sane?"

"Entirely? Who among us is entirely sane?"

"I am," Stone said. "You are."

"You'll have to speak for yourself."

"Why is it I can't get anybody to take a position on Harvey's sanity or character? Not Carrie, not you."

"I've told you, Stone, I don't feel competent to make that judgment."

"And Carrie seems to keep changing her mind."

"A woman's prerogative."

"And an exasperating one, too."

"I think Carrie, in general, seems to want to think the best of everyone, perhaps even Harvey, though of course, she did divorce

133

him, so she must have had *some* doubts about the guy."

"In my experience as an attorney, amicable divorces are rare-to-nonexistent. All too often people seem to want to reduce their exes, not just in wealth but in general well-being. It makes them happier if they can make their exes unhappier."

"I think that's a cynical take on the human race," Nicky said.

"A couple of property division conferences can make a cynic of you."

"I suppose I'm fortunate in my marriage. Vanessa and I have hardly ever had a cross word. That's unusual, I suppose."

"Unusual? It's miraculous."

"I seem to remember that Susannah and her ex had some issues."

"Issues? She shot him in the head."

"In self-defense, of course."

"Of course."

"Do you think she enjoyed doing it?"

"I don't know," Stone said, "but I was around at the time, and she didn't seem to have any regrets."

The party was celebratory, just short of raucous. A jazz trio played in the living room, and outside, at the far end of the deck, a mariachi band of plump men with stringed instruments and sombreros held its cultural own. Ed made a charming little speech about how he had met Susannah; then more meat than Stone had ever seen at one time was served from an outdoor grill that had been trucked in from somewhere or other.

Stone and Gala found a reasonably quiet corner and attacked their steaks, washed down with a spectacular cabernet that somebody kept filling their glasses with.

Ed came over to check on them. "How's it going?" he asked.

"I've already gained two pounds," Stone replied.

"That's the way it should go," Ed said, laughing. "Susannah is enjoying herself." He nodded toward his wife, who was laughing very hard at somebody's joke. "She loves a party, not least when it's in her honor." He wandered on to speak to his other guests.

"Susannah got lucky with that guy," Gala said.

"Nice to know there are some happy marriages," Stone said. "I was having a chat with Nicky Chalmers this afternoon on that same subject, and he puts Vanessa and himself among that group. On the other hand, I have to drive to a place called

Abiquiu tomorrow morning, to make sure that a client's ex-husband isn't doing her in."

"I love it up there," Gala said. "Want some company?"

"I love good company. We'll have Nicky along, too, for a guide."

"You won't need him with me along," she said. "I know the territory."

"Then I'll get the address and we'll ditch him," Stone said.

23

Gala insisted on picking up Stone the following morning in her new Aston Martin.

"You figured out how to drive it?"

"I read the manual," she said, "as a last resort." She pressed the "sport" button and, using the paddles to shift, tore down the mountain and headed northwest, toward Española. A little later they entered a dramatic landscape. "I can understand why O'Keeffe wanted to paint up here," he said.

"This address you have is a cabin at Ghost Ranch," Gala said. "I know the place." They turned off the main highway past signs warning of private property, and after a dusty drive through the surrounding hills, came to a low adobe house — more like a cabin — with a green Range Rover parked outside. "Here you are," Gala said, setting the brake and turning up the jazz on the satellite radio. "I'll wait."

"Give me a few minutes," he said. "If she's

receiving visitors, I'll ask her to invite you in."

"I'm happy here," she said.

Stone got out of the low-slung car and walked to the door, which was ajar. He rapped on the ancient wood. "Carrie? It's Stone Barrington. You here?"

A radio played mariachi music somewhere. "Carrie?" He pushed the door and it swung open to reveal a simple but attractive sitting room. Everything was in perfect order, except that a Toyo 5×7 camera lay on its side, still affixed to its wooden tripod. A dining table held half a dozen pieces of photographic equipment. "Carrie?" he called.

The music seemed to be coming from the next room, probably a bedroom. "Carrie?" he called once again. No response. He looked at his watch: 10:35 AM, a little late for her to still be sleeping. He knocked on the door to the next room and got no response. He opened the door. "Carrie?"

The radio was on a small writing table across the room from the bed. Windows were open, and there was the noise of flies buzzing. Carrie was in the bed, under a spread, her head turned slightly away from him. "Carrie?" He approached her and put a hand on her shoulder. She was unresponsive; she had that inert feeling of a dead person. He put a hand to her throat and felt for a pulse; she was at about room temperature, and there was no pulse. Her eyes were half open, and he closed them.

Stone left the room, then the house. He went to the car and got in, grateful for the air-conditioning in the idling vehicle. He turned the radio off. "What county are we in?" he asked.

"Rio Arriba," Gala replied. "I saw a sign on the road."

He got out his cell phone and dialed 911, wondering if he would be connected to New York's emergency services. The phone was picked up on the first ring. "Rio Arriba Sheriff's Office," a woman said.

"My name is Stone Barrington," Stone said. "May I speak to the sheriff, please? I want to report a homicide."

"Did you say a homicide?"

"Yes."

"Just a minute, I'll see if I can get the sheriff on the radio." He heard her calling and getting an answer. "Hang on, I'll patch you through to Sheriff Martinez."

"This is Ray Martinez," a man said.

"Sheriff, my name is Stone Barrington. I'm at Ghost Ranch, at a small adobe house with the name Casa Juanita."

"I know the place. You say there's a homicide?"

"Yes. I'm an attorney. I came here to visit a client of mine. Her name is Carrie Fiske. I found her in her bed, unresponsive. I should think she's been dead since sometime yesterday."

"I met her yesterday morning when I was on patrol. She was taking pictures. I'm not far away — I'll be there in ten minutes."

"You're going to need a crime scene team and a medical examiner, the works."

"I'll call that in," Martinez said. "Over and out."

Stone ended the call. Gala was staring at him. "Sounds like we're late," she said.

Stone nodded. "I'm afraid this is going to take a few hours. Sorry about that."

"Not to worry. Is it bad in there?"

"No sign of a disturbance, except an overturned camera on a tripod. Everything else is neat as a pin."

"You said it's a homicide — that means not natural causes?"

"That's right."

"How did she die?"

"I'm going to let the sheriff discover that," Stone said. "Policemen everywhere don't like their crime scenes disturbed."

The sheriff was there inside ten minutes, as he had promised, and Stone got out of the car to greet him.

"Mr. Barrington?"

"That's right."

"I'm Ray Martinez." The two men shook hands. "On the phone it sounded like you know what you're talking about."

"I'm a retired NYPD detective," he said.

"Tell me what I've got here."

"I came to see Ms. Fiske. The front door was ajar. I got no response, so I went inside. Everything is in good order, except for a camera on a tripod that may have been knocked over. Ms. Fiske is in her bed, a radio was playing."

"And why do you think it's a homicide?"

"I came here to tell her that her life could be in danger."

"Well, I want to hear all about that," the sheriff said. "First, take me in the way you went and show me what you found."

Stone took him inside and showed him.

Martinez lifted a corner of the spread and found Carrie Fiske, deceased. Her clothing had been disturbed; she was naked from the waist down, and her clothes were near her feet, under the spread.

"Strangled, looks like," Martinez said. "Let's me and you go have a seat. I want to know everything you know."

They went back into the living room, and Stone began to tell him the history of the past couple of weeks, while Martinez took notes.

24

Stone and Sheriff Martinez stood on the front porch of the little house and watched Carrie Fiske's body being loaded into a county ambulance.

"I've requested a statewide APB on this guy, Harvey Biggers," Martinez said. "I've also alerted the Santa Fe and Albuquerque police to cover the airports. The way you describe him, he should be easy to spot."

"I should think so," Stone said. "What did the ME have to say about the cause of death?"

"Strangulation, like I thought. She also had some broken ribs and some defensive bruises on her forearms. Apparently, he sat on her while he killed her. It wasn't pretty."

"It never is, is it?"

"You got that right. Our murders around here generally fall into two big categories — barroom and domestic. I've never had a rich Anglo woman victim, and I've been in office nine years."

"In New York, we got 'em all — rich, poor, and in between."

"Why'd you retire young?" Martinez asked.

"The official reason was that I flunked the physical after a gunshot wound to the knee," Stone replied. "But I think you could say my departure was by popular request."

Martinez emitted a short laugh. "I know what that's like. I was a street cop in Albuquerque," he said, "and I never fitted in too well. My captain called me 'Smartass,' like it was my name. I had to punch a couple of guys who tried to make it that."

The ME walked over to where they stood. "I'll have a report for you tomorrow. The tox screen will take a lot longer, although that wouldn't seem to bear on the case. What difference does it make if she was drunk, doped, or sober? She was murdered all the same." He got into his car and drove away.

"You said you came up here to warn her?" Martinez asked.

"I tried to call her yesterday afternoon, as soon as I heard Biggers was in Santa Fe, but we had a bad cell connection, so I came up here."

"What time did you talk to her?"

"Three-thirty, four o'clock."

"So we know she was alive then."

"If Harvey left Santa Fe before I was looking for him, he could have been here then."

"That falls within the ME's guess. He said late afternoon, early evening."

"The stomach contents will tell you something about that, whether she'd had dinner or not."

"Why wouldn't she tell you where she was?"

"She presented me with a dog for a gift, and I think she was afraid I'd want to return it. She needn't have worried, the dog and I get along just fine."

"Who else knew where she was, except this Nicky guy?"

"Harvey Biggers," Stone said. "But I don't know how he found out or who else knew."

They were driving back. "I was impressed with how calmly you handled that," she said.

"I had a lot of practice when I was on the force. It gets to be routine, except once in a while when you get riled or really interested. This one was very violent, and that makes me angry. Carrie certainly didn't deserve it."

"It could have happened to me, if I'd stuck with the marriage," Gala said. "I was afraid to file for divorce, but I knew I had to just suck it up and get it done, if I wanted to live a long and healthy life."

"Do you still feel that you're in any danger?"

"Not so much. It helps that we're in different cities. I had everything he could have thought he owned packed up and shipped back to L.A., so he wouldn't have an excuse to come out here."

"You sent his belongings to his house?"

"No, I was more considerate than that. I had the shipper store everything, and I wrote and told him. I even paid for the packing and shipping. He was still angry, called me up and started yelling, but I hung up on him."

"How long ago was this?"

"Oh, five or six weeks, I guess. I've occupied myself by shopping for replacement things. It's a pretty big house, so I had a lot to do. Second time I've done it."

"Did you have any trouble getting a settlement?"

"Not really. The California community property laws help keep it simple. It's mostly arguing about which half of things you're going to get. I told my lawyer to settle it with his lawyer, and I guess I was lucky that he had a girlfriend that he wanted to marry, so he didn't make a lot of trouble."

"Did he marry her?"

"Nope. I heard she left him right after the divorce was final. She had the advantage of watching how he handled the divorce, and I think she was able to put herself in my boots. She was an actress. I heard she got an offer to do a play in New York and took it in a heartbeat."

She drove him back to her house. "You got any dinner plans?"

"Nope."

"Good. I'll make us an omelet or something, and then we'll see how it goes."

"I'll need to stop by Ed's house first. I have some bad news to deliver to Nicky and Vanessa Chalmers."

25

They arrived at the Eagle residence at the cocktail hour, and Juan brought them drinks.

Nicky waited until they were served, then asked his question. "Did you see Carrie?"

Stone took a deep breath. "Yes, but I was too late."

"To late for what?"

"To keep her safe."

"You mean . . ."

"Yes. I found her at her house, on the bed. The medical examiner for the county said she had been beaten and strangled."

Nicky's drink slipped from his grasp and spilled on the floor; Juan rushed over with a towel. "If only . . ." he began, then stopped.

"There are always 'if onlys,' " Stone said. "You didn't do anything wrong, just what she asked you to do."

"I heard her voice on the phone, but I couldn't understand her."

"She was probably killed shortly after that. We couldn't have gotten there in time, and even if we'd been able to warn her — well, she'd been warned before."

"Where is Harvey?"

"In the wind. The sheriff up there put out a statewide all-points bulletin on him, and the airports in Santa Fe and Albuquerque are being watched. He could be anywhere."

Ed Eagle spoke for the first time. "Anything I can do to help?"

"If you think of something, let me know, Ed. I've been over it, and I think what can be done is being done. One thing, though — I've got to call Dino. Excuse me." He got up and went into the study.

"Bacchetti."

"It's Stone."

"Where are you? I left a couple of messages."

"I'm in Santa Fe, at Ed Eagle's house."

"What took you out there?"

"Just a getaway. Yesterday was Susannah's birthday, and there was a big party last night. There's a guy named Nicky Chalmers here, a new client of mine and a friend of Carrie Fiske. He was shopping in Santa Fe yesterday and saw Harvey Biggers in the plaza. Nicky finally admitted that Carrie was out here — about fifty miles north, a place called Abiquiu."

"Where Georgia O'Keeffe painted."

"Right. I called her, but the cell service was poor, so I went up there this morning and found her dead."

"Shit."

"Yes, exactly. The police are looking everywhere for Biggers, but I think he's gone. I think it might be a good idea for you to have the airports covered. The guy's about six-six and thickly built. He shouldn't be hard to spot, and it makes sense that he'd go back to New York."

"How long has she been dead?"

"Maybe twenty-four hours."

"If he's coming back here he's had plenty of opportunity to get past the airports, so that would be a waste of time. I'll send some people around to his place — maybe he just went home."

"Could be — it's not as though he's been behaving rationally."

"Give Ed Eagle my best."

"Right. See you." They both hung up, and Stone went back to the living room. "Okay, New York is covered. Nicky, think about this — is there somewhere else where Harvey might run?"

Nicky thought about it, then shook his head. "I don't know him well enough to know where that would be."

"Do you know if he has any family?"

"Not that I'm aware of. Neither does Carrie, for that matter."

"He probably has a rental car," Ed said. "He could have just continued north to Denver. He could fly just about anywhere from there."

"Nicky, did Carrie own any other properties other than New York and East Hampton?"

"She has a house in Palm Beach, on Ocean Drive."

"Does anybody live there when she's away?"

Nicky shook his head. "Just a housekeeper, but she's not a live-in."

Stone's cell phone rang, but the calling number was blocked. "Hello?"

"Is this Stone Barrington?" A woman's voice.

"Yes."

"This is Monique Sullivan, at CNN. I'm calling about the death of Carrie Fiske, and I understand you're her attorney."

"Hang on a minute. Excuse me, I'd better take this."

He walked into the study. "Ms. Sullivan?"

"Yes. Can you tell me what happened? And don't spare the details."

"You should call Sheriff Martinez at the Rio Arriba Sheriff's Office. He's the man in charge."

"I've already spoken to him, and he didn't give me much. All I know is she's dead and they're looking for her ex-husband, one Harvey Biggert."

"Biggers. That's what I know, too. It would be helpful if you could report that on the air."

"Love to, but I need details. Where are you right now?"

"I'm in Santa Fe."

"Great, so am I. Could we meet for a drink?"

"I'm sorry, I'm spending the evening with friends. You can call me tomorrow. Goodbye." He hung up, and his phone began to ring again, almost immediately. He switched it off and put it back into his holster.

26

They had dinner with the Eagles, then Gala went home. "Call me tomorrow," she said to Stone as she left.

Stone awoke the following morning to the ringing of his cell phone. "Hello?"

"It's Joan."

"Why so early?"

"It's nine o'clock in the morning."

"Not in Santa Fe."

"Oh, well, you're up at seven every morning anyway."

"What is it?"

"Your new client, Ms. Fiske?"

"Yes?"

"You did a will for her, remember?"

"Yes, and we sent it to her a few days ago."

"Well, she executed it — properly, I might add. All the signatures in the right places — but she made a change at the end."

"What was that?"

"She crossed out the name of the bank

she had named as executor, and wrote in your name and initialed it."

"Oh, shit, that's a job I don't want."

"Well, you can always get her to change it."

"I'm afraid not — she died the day before yesterday."

"Uh-oh, the husband?"

"Highly likely. If he turns up, don't let him in and call the cops. Try not to shoot him."

"Whatever you say. When are you coming home?"

"I was coming home today, but now I have arrangements to make. I forget, did she name a burial place?"

"Palm Beach, in her back garden, next to her parents."

"Got an address?"

"It's on Ocean Drive." She gave him the number.

"All right." He hung up, shaved, showered, and dressed and went down to breakfast. Nicky and Vanessa were already there. Stone greeted them, sat down, and reached for the eggs.

"I got a phone call this morning from my secretary. Carrie executed the will I drew up for her, but she changed the executor from her bank to me."

"From your mien, I take it that's a job you don't want."

"You are correct. You have a place in Palm Beach, as I recall."

"That's right."

"Carrie expressed a wish to be buried in her garden there."

"Yes, I remember that her parents are buried in a plot there."

"Can you recommend a funeral director in Palm Beach?"

Nicky came up with a name. "That's the society gravedigger, which means it will cost three times as much as it would in West Palm Beach, but Carrie would expect you to use them."

Ed and Susannah came in. "I heard that last part. You're her executor?" Ed asked.

"I'm afraid so. Can you recommend a funeral director here to collect the body and ship it?"

"Sure." He wrote down a name and gave it to Stone.

"Is the estate going to have to go to probate?"

"No, I drew up a revocable trust for her."

"I'll order some certified copies of the death certificates for you. How many do you want?"

"I don't know, fifty? I've handled exactly

one estate since Arrington's death, and I needed that many then."

"I'll send somebody over from my office to collect them. I'll speak to the ME, too. I can't see any reason why he shouldn't release the body immediately, since there's no doubt about the cause of death."

"Thanks. Could you FedEx them to New York? Looks as though I'll be making a stop in Palm Beach before going home. Nicky, if you want to be there for the burial, I'll be happy to have you fly with me, then back to New York, if that's where you're headed."

"Thank you, Stone, we'd like to be there, and we appreciate the ride."

Stone finished his breakfast then went into Ed's study and started making calls. Inside an hour he had made the necessary arrangements, received a faxed copy of the will from Joan, and was packed and ready to go. He called Gala.

"Hello?"

"Good morning," he said.

"You aren't going home today, are you?"

Stone explained his new duties. "How would you like a free trip to Palm Beach and New York for a few days?"

"I think I could handle that."

"Pick you up in an hour?"

"What shall I pack?"

"Something for a funeral, and whatever else you would like."

"I think I'll travel light. I haven't been shopping in New York for a long time. In an hour, then."

Stone said goodbye to Susannah. "I don't remember if I wished you a happy birthday."

"Neither do I," she replied. "It was that kind of party."

"I'm grateful for the introduction to Gala."

"So is she. Take good care of her, she needs it."

"Certainly."

Ed drove them to the airport, picking up Gala on the way. He had a good look at Stone's airplane and approved. They shook hands.

"Your turn to come to New York," Stone said.

"We'll surprise you."

"I'll count on that."

Stone had filed direct to Palm Beach International, and half an hour later they were at flight level 410, with a stiff tailwind.

27

Stone landed at Palm Beach International and got a rental car. Nicky had arranged for him and Vanessa to be picked up. "I called Carrie's housekeeper as you requested," he said, handing Stone a slip of paper. "You and Gala are perfectly welcome to stay with us."

"Thank you, but I suppose I'm going to have to dispose of Carrie's house, so I'd better have a look at it."

Nicky took out a notepad and wrote down another number. "Here's a local man, an antiques dealer, who specializes in selling estate property, and the name of a real estate agent you might consider for selling the house."

"Thank you, Nicky. I'll call you as soon as I hear from the undertaker and have a time for the service."

They shook hands and departed. Bob, who had been waiting patiently, hopped into the backseat and looked for an open window. Stone knew where Ocean Drive was and got them there, while Gala watched for the house number. "There!" she said. "The next one."

Stone pulled into a gated drive; the gate was open, and they passed through. The house was set well back from the road; it was Georgian in style and reminded him of his property in England. He drove up, and a woman in a black uniform and white apron came out the front door and greeted them.

"I'm Hazel Sizemore," she said, "the housekeeper here. I expect you're Mr. Barrington?"

"That's right," Stone said, shaking her hand. "And this is Ms. Wilde." A man in a black suit emerged from the house and took their luggage from the car. He was introduced as Oscar. "I know this must have come as a shock to you, Ms. Sizemore."

"Hazel, please. Well, it did and it didn't come as a surprise. I always thought that Mr. Biggers might harm her. Mr. Chalmers explained everything on the phone, and the undertaker has already called. His number is by the phone on the hall table. I've put you in the Magnolia Suite — that's our nicest guest room."

"Thank you, that's very kind. We'll try not to be too much trouble."

"Oh, it's no trouble. Ms. Fiske always asked us to be ready for guests at any time. What time would you like dinner?"

"Say, seven-thirty?"

"Is there anything in particular you'd like?"

"No, whatever is convenient for you."

"As you wish. May I give you a little tour?"

"Thank you, yes." Hazel led them into a large drawing room that had had the attention of a very fine decorator, followed by a library, a billiards room, small and large dining rooms, and a broad rear roofed terrace that looked out over the extensive gardens, with Lake Worth at the end.

"Ms. Fiske had one of the few properties that run from the ocean to the lake," Hazel said. "Her grandfather built it, and her father put in the dock and boathouse. It's fenced in, if you'd like to let the dog out."

Bob, delighted to be off his lead, began a systematic inspection of the gardens.

"It's all very beautiful," Stone said. He stopped at the hall table and called the undertaker, a Mr. Willis.

"Thank you for returning my call, Mr. Barrington," he said. "I've received word that Ms. Fiske's remains have arrived in

Atlanta and will be put on an early-morning airplane tomorrow and will arrive in Palm Beach around mid-morning. When would you like to have the burial?"

"Would tomorrow afternoon be convenient?"

"We have some work to do beforehand — say, four PM?"

"That will be fine."

"You may leave the choice of flowers and a minister to us, if you like."

"That's fine."

"There remains only the choice of the coffin. Would you like to come to our showroom?"

"Have you something in mahogany?" Stone asked, remembering the last time he had viewed coffins.

"We do. We have a very fine model — solid mahogany with a silk lining at sixty-nine thousand dollars. That price includes the shipping of the remains and all our work, the preparation of the burial site, with which we are familiar from the burial of Ms. Fiske's parents, and a simple headstone with her dates, which we have. Is there some sentiment you'd like included?"

"I think not. I'm sure the coffin will be suitable."

"Our people will arrive early tomorrow

161

morning to prepare the gravesite. They will try not to disturb you."

"Thank you, Mr. Willis."

Stone whistled up Bob, and he and Gala followed Hazel upstairs to a large sitting room, with a bedroom and bath to one side. The view was of the gardens and the lake.

Stone thanked her, and they spent a few minutes hanging up their clothes.

"There is a lot of very fine American antique furniture in this house," Gala said. "I mean, stuff that would bring millions at auction."

"I thought there were some very good pieces," Stone said.

"Virtually every bit of wood furniture we've seen," Gala said, stroking a chest of drawers in the room. "I expect that her grandparents and parents must have bought most of it many years ago, before the prices skyrocketed. There are some valuable pictures, too. I swear I spotted a Rembrandt downstairs."

"I handled the estate of a good friend a while back," Stone said. "He had a lot of very fine things and a big art collection. I was fortunate, as executor, that his house was preserved pretty much intact, and I didn't have to dispose of the contents. This one is going to be different, I fear."

"I think you'll have to have everything very carefully cataloged and appraised."

"Yes, and I know just who to bring in for that."

"In the meantime, we have a day to enjoy the place," Gala said. "Do you feel like a nap?"

"Not really."

"Neither do I," she said, kissing him.

28

Stone and Gala, fresh from making love and showering together, dined in the small dining room, where Hazel had set a beautiful table with old Wedgwood and Baccarat crystal and had put out a selection of wines from the cellar, from which Stone chose a Château Palmer '61, a claret Stone had heard much of but never tasted. Oscar decanted it, and it surpassed what Stone could have hoped for.

"This is such a beautiful place," Gala said. "It seems a shame to pull it apart and sell everything off piecemeal."

"As Carrie's executor, I would be delighted to sell it to you intact."

She laughed. "Would that I could afford it."

"The problem with a house like this is that the only people who could afford it are people you wouldn't want living next door."

"I know what you mean — people like my

ex-husband, not that he could afford it, either. What do you think it might sell for?"

"I wouldn't know what to ask," Stone said.

"Tell you what, I'll think about it and make you an offer."

"I will look forward to receiving it."

They were served seared foie gras, followed by a *suprême de volaille* with a tarragon cream sauce, which went very well with the wine. When Hazel came back he asked her if she was the chef.

"Oh, no, sir, that would be Bonnie, who has been with the family for more than thirty years."

"And how long have you been here?"

"I'm a newcomer — only twenty-seven years. Oscar has been here for fifteen."

"How many others on staff?"

"Three housemaids and two gardeners, with occasional extra help from outside."

"It seems to be a tightly run ship."

"We try." She took away their plates, then served a peach cobbler with half a bottle of Château d'Yquem 1978.

"Heavenly," Gala said.

They took Bob for a stroll in the gardens after dinner, then retired early, in each other's arms. Bob slept on a large pillow next to their bed.

■ ■ ■ ■

Stone was awakened shortly after seven AM by the sound of some sort of industrial engine running. He went to the window and peeked through the curtain.

"What is it?" Gala asked sleepily.

"A backhoe, digging the grave. It shouldn't take long." It didn't, and they called down for breakfast in bed, which arrived with the *New York Times* and the *Wall Street Journal.*

Nicky called at mid-morning to check on the time of the service and invite them to his place for dinner.

Nicky and Vanessa arrived at three-thirty and were given a glass of champagne, then at four o'clock, they walked out into the garden and stood at the graveside. An Episcopal minister read a psalm and said a prayer, and the coffin was lowered into the earth. As they turned from the grave, Stone saw a young woman standing a few yards away. Thinking she might have been a friend of Carrie's, he walked over and introduced himself.

"I'm Monique Sullivan," she said. "We spoke on the phone in Santa Fe. From CNN, remember?. May I speak to you now?"

"Ms. Sullivan, I admire your enterprise, but we've just concluded a burial service here."

"I won't take much of your time," she said.

He turned to the others. "Go on inside, I'll be along in a minute." He directed the young reporter to a garden bench, and they sat down. "All right, you've got five minutes." He glanced at his watch.

She quickly reviewed the facts of the case, and he confirmed them. "Are you satisfied that she was murdered by her ex-husband, Harvey Biggers?"

"Mr. Biggers seems to be a person of interest," Stone replied, "though he hasn't been charged with anything."

"Your opinion?"

"I'll reserve my judgment until I've heard all the evidence."

"What, in your personal experience, would make Mr. Biggers a suspect?"

"He had threatened her in the past, and he has been a presence in the investigation of the deaths of two other women."

"What do you mean by 'a presence'?"

"He was in their company shortly before they died, both under unexplained circumstances. That's three things that would make him interesting to a homicide investigator."

"I suppose so. What evidence is there that

Biggers was in Abiquiu at the time of Ms. Fiske's death?"

"He was seen in Santa Fe by someone who knew him well, the afternoon before her death."

Stone glanced at his watch.

"Just one more question."

"All right."

"Who is the man who watched the funeral from a third-floor window?"

"What?"

She pointed, and he followed her finger, but all he saw was the movement of a curtain. Stone got up and started running toward the house.

29

Stone ran up the stone stairs to the rear of the house and into the downstairs hall, past Nicky, Vanessa, and Gala, who stood chatting. It occurred to him that he was unarmed, so as he passed a hall stand he grabbed a sturdy golf umbrella.

He ran up the main stairs to the third floor, which he had not yet visited, and began opening doors to rooms with a view of the rear gardens. He got lucky on the second one.

It was a smaller guest room than the one he was occupying a floor down; the bed was unmade, and there were a couple of men's suits and a jacket or two in an open closet. Two drawers of a chest were open, one of them filled with dirty laundry. But where was the occupant? He stood still and listened for a moment, trying to slow his heavy breathing from the run up the stairs.

He heard a heavy footstep from the south

end of the house and the sound of a door slamming and feet on gravel. He could see no one out the back window, so he ran across the hall to a front bedroom and pulled up the blinds. He saw a large male figure carrying a suitcase turn a curve in the driveway and disappear in the direction of Ocean Drive.

He grabbed his phone and dialed 911, then thought better of it. Instead, he called Dino. It took a moment for the secretary to put him through, and he used it to get his heart and breathing rate down.

"Bacchetti."

"It's Stone. Please listen carefully. I'm in Palm Beach, where we have just buried Carrie Fiske." He gave Dino the address. "I don't know if there's an APB out for Harvey Biggers down here, and the Palm Beach police don't know me. Biggers was watching the burial from a third-floor bedroom, where he seems to have been living for a couple of days. He just ran out of the house toward Ocean Drive, and he probably has a car parked someplace nearby. Will you call the chief down here and get his people on it?"

"Yeah, okay. You're sure it was Biggers?"

"He was as big as Biggers, and who the hell else could he be?"

170

"Why would he be there?"

"I think, maybe, he wanted to attend Carrie's funeral, but didn't want to see me."

"All right. I'll call you back." They both hung up.

Stone walked slowly down the stairs to the hall and found his three companions staring at him. "Harvey was watching the burial from the third floor," he said. "He got out in a hurry. The police will be here soon."

"Excuse me," said a female voice behind him. He turned to find Monique Sullivan standing in the rear doorway. "May I come in?"

"Yes, do. Everybody, this is Ms. Monique Sullivan, of CNN. This is Mr. and Mrs. Chalmers and Ms. Wilde."

Everyone murmured a greeting.

"Was that Harvey Biggers watching from upstairs?"

"I believe so. He seems to have been living up there for a couple of days."

"Over us?" Gala asked.

"More or less. He ran when he heard me coming up the stairs."

"What's the umbrella for?" Vanessa asked.

"Persuasion," Stone said, dropping it back into the umbrella stand.

"Did you persuade him of anything?"

"Just to leave, I guess."

"Shouldn't we call the police?" Nicky asked.

"I've already done that." As if on cue they heard tires on gravel from the front drive. "I guess they don't use sirens in good neighborhoods."

The doorbell rang, and Stone opened it. Two uniformed patrolmen stood in the doorway, their caps in their hands.

"Mr. Barrington?"

"Yes, I am."

"We got a call about an intruder in the house?"

"He left by the front door. Did you see anyone afoot on Ocean Drive?"

"You mean South Ocean Boulevard?"

"I do."

"No, sir, just cars. We understood that the person is a suspect in a murder?"

"That's correct."

"Name of Harvey Biggers?"

"Correct again."

"The chief has already given the order to close the bridges. Not close them, exactly, but we've got a description, and officers are looking into every car driving off the island."

"That's the advantage of policing an island, I guess," Stone said.

"Yes, sir. Did the man do any damage here?"

"No, but he slept here for a couple of nights, in a bedroom on the third floor, top of the stairs, second on the left."

"May we take a look?"

"Go right ahead."

The two policemen trotted up the stairs.

"Nicky," Stone said, "might Harvey try to take shelter at your house?"

"Well, he knows where we live — he came there with Carrie for dinner on a few occasions. We'll be real careful when we get home. Can you and Gala come about seven for dinner? We'll be real casual, no neckties."

"Thank you, yes."

The Chalmerses left to go home.

Hazel appeared in the downstairs hall. "Mr. Barrington, did I just see two policemen going upstairs?"

"Yes, you did, Hazel. Apparently Mr. Biggers has been sleeping in a third-floor bedroom for a couple of nights."

Her hand flew to her mouth. "Oh, my goodness. Nobody has been up there since the first of the week. Are we in any danger?"

"No, he fled when discovered, and the police are looking for him now. Don't worry, he won't be back."

"Thank God for that," she said. "The housemaids will be in tomorrow morning, and I'll have them tidy up."

"Thank you, Hazel. We'll be dining out tonight, and we'll be on our way to New York tomorrow morning."

"Yes, Mr. Barrington. What time would you like breakfast?"

"Seven o'clock will be fine." She went back toward the kitchen.

Gala came and leaned against Stone. "I didn't think this trip would be nearly so exciting."

"Neither did I," Stone replied.

30

Nicky and Vanessa Chalmers lived in a tony neighborhood, but with much smaller houses than those on South Ocean Boulevard. Stone and Gala turned up on time and were given a drink out back, beside a small swimming pool. Stone sipped his Knob Creek, and Gala had a martini.

"It's been quite a few days, hasn't it?" Nicky observed.

"No argument there," Stone replied.

A uniformed maid came out to where they sat. "Excuse me, Mr. Chalmers, but you might want to turn on the TV, to CNN."

Nicky reached for the remote and turned it on. They were watching an aerial shot, apparently from a helicopter or a drone, and the voice of Monique Sullivan could be heard. "The Fiske estate, one of the oldest on South Ocean Boulevard in Palm Beach, is one of the oldest and most elegant of the mansions lining the beachfront." As she spoke the camera began to zoom in, until it was possible to make out two figures sitting on a bench in the Fiske garden.

"That's us," Stone said, amazed. He could now recognize himself and Sullivan, as she interviewed him, and the sound was perfect.

"You mean that conversation is being recorded by somebody in the air?"

"Must have been a drone," Stone said. "I didn't hear a chopper, and there were no cameras around us. That's very sneaky." He saw Sullivan point at the house, and the shot zoomed in on the upstairs window, just as a figure moved behind a curtain.

"That was Harvey," Nicky said. "I'd recognize him anywhere."

"It was a pretty brief glimpse, Nicky," Stone said. "Are you sure?"

"I am."

A moment later the camera caught a figure running from the house and began to zoom in again, losing him as he ran behind some shrubbery along the driveway. The man, who was carrying a suitcase, ran out to the boulevard, then made two lefts into side streets, got into a dark car, and made his escape. The camera didn't follow him.

"The television arts seem to have made great technical advances when I wasn't looking," Stone said.

"Well, they say you can't go anywhere without being on camera," Nicky observed.

They finished a good dinner and were on coffee in Nicky's study when he brought up a new subject. "Stone, have you given any thought as to what Carrie's house is worth?"

"Not really. I'm going to have to order appraisals of the house and its contents."

"The same with the East Hampton house and the New York apartment, I suppose."

"I expect so. I've seen the East Hampton house, of course, but what is the New York apartment like?"

"A duplex at 740 Park Avenue, which is said to be the best building in the city."

"I've heard that."

"Vanessa and I were talking this afternoon. We've never put a great deal of money into our residences, partly because we didn't want the bother of decorating them. We didn't have the sort of eye that Carrie had, and it occurs to us that, well . . ." He gathered himself. "I'd like to make you, or rather, the estate, an offer."

"For the Palm Beach house?"

"For all three properties."

"God, that's a very large bite, Nicky."

"I'm aware of that. Fortunately, I have a very large fortune. My father died a few months ago, and it got even larger. I know that you'll have to get appraisals done, but I'd like to offer the estate a hundred million dollars for all three of Carrie's properties."

"That's a breathtaking offer, Nicky, but of course I'll have to get appraisals of not only the properties but of the contents. Carrie had a lot of fine art in the Palm Beach house and a lot of American antique furniture, as well, much of which would bring large numbers at auction."

"I understand, and I'm prepared to adjust my offer, if necessary, when the appraisals come in. We might exclude some of the pieces, which you could auction."

"Well, when I get back to New York, I'll get people to work on that. As long as you understand that my duty as executor is to get market prices."

"Having been through it with my father's estate, I'm well aware of the hoops you have to jump through."

"Yes, and it would simplify life for me if I could sell it all to one buyer. I'll give you, unofficially, a first option."

"That's all I could ask for," Nicky said.

Driving home, Gala spoke up. "Does Nicky really have that kind of money?"

"He does. His great-grandfather founded,

at the dawn of the automobile age, what became the largest tire company in the United States, perhaps in the world, and the family, that is to say, Nicky, still owns a majority of it. He has recently become a client of my firm, so I'm familiar with the facts of the matter."

"I was just thinking," Gala said, "the real estate could give Nicky an excellent motive for, well . . ."

"Nicky a murderer? Come on, you've gotten to know him, do you think he would be capable of that?"

"Well, as he said, it's an opportunity for him to acquire not just Carrie's real estate, but her taste, as it were."

"You have an evil mind," Stone said.

"I was married to an evil man for eight years," she said.

They walked Bob in the garden, then went to bed, but Gala's thoughts about Nicky kept him awake for a while.

31

Nicky called the following morning and said that he and Vanessa had decided to spend a few more days in Palm Beach, so they wouldn't be flying to New York with Stone and Gala.

They had an uneventful flight to Teterboro, emptied Bob on arrival, and Fred met them and drove them into the city.

"Well," Gala said, looking around Stone's living room, "it's more masculine than Carrie's house, but it's very nice indeed. It looks like you, so my guess is that you were your own interior decorator."

"Good guess," Stone said. He installed her in the master suite and left her working at her laptop.

Bob was very happy to see Joan, as she was the source of many cookies.

"I was afraid you'd make him fat on your trip," she said to Stone.

"He's in more danger of that around you," Stone replied.

"So, I guess we're in for another bout of estate settling," Joan commented.

"Yes, we are."

"I thought that, after dealing with Eduardo Bianchi's estate, I'd never have to do that again until you fell off the twig."

"Don't worry, I'll see that Woodman & Weld do a full-court press. The main thing is to get the valuations of the real estate done. Call those people who did Eduardo's house and get them on the job."

"Right."

Stone sat down at his desk and started to go through the mail and messages, then Dino called.

"Welcome back."

"Thanks. What do you hear from the Palm Beach cops?"

"They failed to bag Biggers."

"I thought when they sealed off the island they'd spot him."

"No such luck. We've got somebody on his apartment building, but no luck so far. Dinner tonight?"

"Let's make it tomorrow night. I brought Susannah Wilde's sister back with me — you'll like her."

"I like them all, Stone, it's just that they

don't like you for very long."

"That's a dirty Communist lie."

"Then why do they keep dumping you?"

"I'm just too much trouble, too set in my ways. See you tomorrow night." He hung up, and Joan buzzed.

"You won't believe who's on line two," she said.

"Do I have to guess?"

"Just pick up."

Stone pressed the button.

"Good morning," a familiar voice said.

"Harvey?"

"I thought that was a very nice service you had for Carrie. And I appreciate the bed. I didn't think I should check into a hotel."

Stone buzzed Joan, and he mouthed, *Get Dino to trace this.* "I guess not," he said to Biggers.

"So, counselor, now that Carrie is gone, you have no conflict with representing me, do you?"

"Just a deep moral conflict," Stone replied. "But, without actually representing you, I'll give you some very good advice."

"And what's that?"

"Turn yourself in."

"But I'm an innocent man."

"All the more reason. Get everything straightened out, then resume your life."

"And it's going to be a very nice life."

"Harvey, you seem to be laboring under the misapprehension that you are still in Carrie's will."

"Of course I am — she didn't have time to change it."

"On the contrary, I drew a new will for her, and she swiftly executed it. I think I can tell you, without violating a confidence, that the only mention of your name in the document is a statement excluding you from inheriting any part of the estate."

"The bitch! I'll contest it!"

"You don't have a leg to stand on. You're divorced, you agreed to and were paid a generous settlement, and then she changed her will. No attorney in the United States would take your case under those circumstances." This was not strictly true, Stone knew, but he wanted to be emphatic.

"Well, that's a disappointment."

"There's also the matter of your murdering her, which would prevent you from inheriting, even if you were still in the will."

"But I didn't murder her!"

"Then that's exactly what you should tell the police when you have your inevitable chat with them."

"I suppose you'd be glad to arrange that."

"I'd be delighted. Where can I get in touch

with you?"

"I think it's best that I stay on the move."

"Harvey, do you have any idea what you're up against? Three police forces, one of them the largest in the world, have made your arrest a top priority, and you have no idea what they can bring to bear on that."

"I watch enough TV to make a pretty good guess," Harvey said. "And that reminds me, I should hang up now or you'll trace my call. Maybe I'll be in touch." He hung up.

Stone hung up, too, and Joan came in, shaking her head. "It was a cell call from somewhere outside the city. There wasn't time to figure out where. We're not expecting another visit from Mr. Biggers, are we?"

"Not likely."

32

Stone and Gala had breakfast in bed the following morning.

"I'm going up to Carrie Fiske's apartment this morning to look it over," Stone said "Would you like to come along?"

"Yes. Do you have a key?"

"Sheriff Martinez sent her luggage from the Ghost Ranch house," Stone said. "Her handbag was among her effects, and there were keys to her properties."

"I'd love to see it."

They arrived at the Park Avenue building at mid-morning; Stone identified himself to the building's superintendent, and they were allowed to enter the apartment.

"How long did Ms. Fiske own the apartment?" Stone asked the man.

"Her grandfather was the original owner," he replied. "Her parents lived here, too, part of the time, and she owned it since their deaths a few years ago. I'll leave you to look around, Mr. Barrington."

Stone and Gala wandered around the rooms, Gala pointing out various pieces of furniture and art. They went upstairs to where the four bedrooms were and went into the master. "That's a Klimt, I believe," Gala said, indicating a large painting on the wall over a dressing table. She opened a large art book on the dressing table and found the picture. "There you are. A pity it's not *The Woman in Gold.*"

They went into Carrie's dressing room, which was very large. "Goodness, what a wardrobe!" Gala said, looking through the dresses. "I believe some of these things must have belonged to her grandmother and mother."

Stone leaned against a panel, and it gave a little, then sprang open, revealing a large safe with an electronic keypad lock. "This looks custom-made," he said. He dug into his pocket and found the key to the apartment. On the same ring was a gold tag with a number engraved on it.

"Is that the combination?" Gala asked.

"Two-two-seven-seven-four-three," Stone read from the tag. "Those numbers, converted to letters, spell 'Carrie.' " He tapped the numbers into the keypad and spun the safe's wheel: the door opened. "It's just a large jewelry box," Stone said. He pulled out a couple of trays to reveal pairs of earrings and some rings.

"I think you should auction these pieces individually," Gala said. She pulled out the bottom tray and gasped.

"What is it?"

Gala picked up the piece: it was a high choker made of diamonds and rubies. "I don't believe it."

"What don't you believe?"

Carrie took him by the hand and led him back into the bedroom, where she flipped through the pages of the Klimt book until she found the portrait she was looking for.

The Woman in Gold," Stone said. "I've seen it at the Neue Galerie."

Gala pointed at the necklace in the portrait. "Look at this," she said, holding up the choker next to the portrait. "Did you see the film about the painting?"

"No."

"Along with this portrait and other Klimts, the Nazis stole this choker from the family, and it ended up on the neck of Mrs. Hermann Goering."

"You think it's the real thing?"

"Let's go back to the safe." She led him back to the dressing room and opened a small door inside the safe. There was a stack of papers inside, and Gala riffed through them. "Receipts," she said, "some of them going back to the twenties." She pulled out a yellowed envelope, which bore the legend *Bijoux Blume, Rue St.-Honoré, Paris.* "How's your French?" she asked.

"Poor."

"I'll translate — it was sold to one A. L. Fiske, in 1946. It was made by Blume from the original design drawings of the choker depicted in Klimt's *Woman in Gold.* The diamonds are all certified as flawless, as are the rubies."

"Do you suppose the jeweler is still there?"

Gala produced her iPhone and Googled the shop. "No mention of it. This receipt is dated more than sixty years ago."

"I've never seen anything quite like it," Stone said. "Does anybody know where the original necklace is?"

Gala did some more Googling. "Apparently, the last time it was seen, Mrs. Goering was wearing it." She read on. "As the Russians approached Carinhall, Goering's hunting lodge, he removed his belongings and burned the place to the ground. I wonder where he took them?"

"That would have been right at the end of the war," Stone said. "I don't think he would have taken them to Berlin."

"Switzerland," Gala said. "I'll bet he got everything to Switzerland." She read on. "Goering was Hitler's deputy and was supposed to succeed him on his death. He sent Hitler a message saying that, if he didn't hear from him shortly, he would assume command of the Reich in Hitler's name, as Hitler had earlier provided. Martin Bormann intercepted the message and convinced Hitler that Goering was attempting a coup, so in his will, Hitler dismissed Goering from all his posts. Goering had fled to his retreat on the Obersalzberg, and he was then moved to Radstadt, near Salzburg, in Austria, where he was arrested by the U.S. Army. There's no mention of his personal property."

Stone looked carefully at the necklace. "There's something engraved here, but it's too small for my eyes."

Gala peered at it. "Mine too."

Stone found a small velvet bag in the safe and dropped the choker into it and put it into his jacket pocket. He pocketed the Blume receipt, as well.

"Let's get out of here," he said, closing the safe and spinning the wheel. As they emerged from the elevator the man at the desk motioned him over.

189

"Ms. Fiske's former husband was just here," he said. "He wanted to collect some of his things from the apartment. I told him you were here, and he said he'd come back later."

"If Mr. Biggers returns, please deny him entrance to the apartment, then call the police and tell them he was here. I am Ms. Fiske's executor, and you are not to admit anyone to the apartment without written permission from me." He gave the man his card. "Let's go," he said to Carrie.

33

They got into a cab, and Stone got out his cell phone. "Excuse me a moment, I've got to call my security guy." He pressed the speed dial and waited.

"Bob Cantor."

"Bob, it's Stone Barrington."

"What do you need?"

"I need you to go to the following address." Stone read it to him. "I want the locks to all the exterior doors rekeyed, and make sure you find all of them on both floors. Got it?"

"Got it."

"You can leave one key with the super, and tell him he's not to admit anyone without written permission from me. Also, check out the security system, then call the managing company and change the entry and exit codes to the number 1946. Also, change the cancellation code, in the event of a false alarm, to Bob."

"Like my name?"

"Sort of."

"How many keys you want?"

"Send me a dozen. Then I want you to go to East Hampton." He gave him the address of the beach house. "Stop by my place on your way, and Joan will give you keys to both properties and a letter of authorization."

"Okay."

"You know somebody who does what you do in Palm Beach, Florida?"

"Yeah, I do."

"Same instructions to him." He gave Bob the address. "The housekeeper's name is Hazel, and he can give three keys to her, then FedEx another dozen to me. Joan will call Hazel and let her know he's coming. And get it done fast, will you?"

"Don't I always?"

"Thanks, Bob." Stone hung up, then looked up a number in his list of contacts and called it.

"Paul Eckstein."

"Paul, it's Stone Barrington."

"How are you, Stone?"

"Very well, thanks. I have a very large appraisal and cataloging assignment for you."

"As large as the Bianchi estate?"

"Larger. Can you come to my house this

morning? I'll give you the details."

"Certainly. I can be there in an hour."

"That's fine. And Paul, please bring a loupe with you."

"I never go anywhere without one."

Stone hung up. "Now we'll get this show on the road."

Back at his office, Stone buzzed Joan. "Please print me up a hundred letterheads, 'The Estate of Carrie Fiske,' using this address and adding my name as executor and trustee." He gave her the keys to the apartment and beach house. "Bob Cantor will be here soon. Give these to him. Paul Eckstein will be here, too. Send him in. And write me two 'To Whom It May Concern' letters, mentioning Bob in one and Paul and his assignees in the other, saying that they are authorized to be admitted to the Fiske premises on my authority as executor."

Joan went back to her office.

"Well, if you'll excuse me," Gala said, "I have a screenplay to work on."

"I'll send you up some lunch later."

She vanished into the elevator.

Bob Cantor arrived, picked up the keys and his letter, and left. Paul Eckstein was right on his heels.

"Come in, Paul, and have a seat."

Eckstein did so. "Well, what do you have for me? I'm all excited."

"Does the name Carrie Fiske ring a bell?"

"Vaguely. Socialite?"

"In a big way. She was murdered near Santa Fe a few days ago, and she was my client."

"Murdered? By whom?"

"The principal suspect is her ex-husband, Harvey Biggers."

"That rings a faint bell, too. Financial guy, very big?"

"Yes."

"Carrie had three residences." He handed Paul a sheet of paper with the addresses. "The East Hampton house is about what you'd expect around Georgica Pond. There's some good contemporary art — I saw a couple of very nice Hockneys — but the Palm Beach and New York residences, as you can tell by the addresses, are prime, and the contents of each contain the collections of three generations, and are something to behold — furniture, silver, jewelry, and art. I want the three appraisals as furnished, but I want to have the option of auctioning an impressive number of pieces of American antique furniture and the better paintings, so make separate appraisals of each."

"How soon do you need this?"

"How fast can you get it done?"

"The East Hampton house, a week. The Palm Beach and New York places, two weeks, if I use a separate team for each place."

"And that would cost the same as if one team took five weeks?"

"Yes, except for any travel expenses. I'll consult with real estate agencies on property values, but I'll want my own people to do the interiors, and I'll want museum and auction house people for the art."

"I'll have keys to all three properties sent to you within twenty-four hours." Joan came in with the authorization letter, and Stone signed it and gave it to Eckstein, who read it.

"This will do nicely."

"Something else." He took the velvet bag from his pocket and placed it in Paul's hand.

Paul weighed it. "Heavy. What is it?"

"That's what I want you to tell me."

34

Paul Eckstein shook the bag, and the contents fell into his hand. He stared at it for a moment, then reached over and pointed Stone's desk lamp at the necklace. He retrieved a loupe from his pocket and examined, randomly, a number of the stones. "These are very good," he said.

Stone took the Blume receipt from his pocket and handed it to Paul. "This says they're all flawless."

Paul read the letter. "Oh, the necklace is a copy — for a minute there, my heart was in my mouth." He looked at some of the rubies. "Mind you, it's an excellent copy, by the original maker."

"What's it worth?"

"At auction, a couple of million dollars, maybe more, if you get a couple of enthusiasts bidding."

"There's a tiny stamp inside the choker," Stone said. "I couldn't make it out."

Paul held the piece close to the lamp, located it, and looked at it through his loupe. "Jesus Christ," he said, and there was wonder in his voice.

"What does it say?"

"It says, 'Bijoux Blume, Paris 1899.' "

"The receipt says 1946."

"Then either the receipt or the necklace is lying."

"Which one?"

"Stone, do you know what this is, or what it's a copy of?"

"Sort of. It's very like the choker in Gustav Klimt's *Woman in Gold.*"

"Its proper title is *Portrait of Adele Bloch-Bauer,* painted in 1907 — or rather, finished in that year. Klimt worked on it for three years before that."

"Yes, I saw it at the Neue Galerie a while back."

"The painting, along with several others, and the choker, were confiscated by the Gestapo shortly after the Anschluss, the Nazi takeover of Austria."

"I know."

"The paintings ended up in the Belvedere Museum, in Vienna. Frau Bloch-Bauer's niece sued the Austrian government, took them all the way to the Supreme Court, then went to arbitration to get them back."

"I know. What happened to the necklace?"

"It ended up in the possession of Hermann Goering. His wife wore it."

"What happened to it at the end of the war?"

"Goering took his possessions out of his hunting lodge, called Carinhall, after his late first wife. As the Russian Army approached, he set fire to the house, and it burned to the ground, then he escaped to his house on the Obersalzberg, the Bavarian Alps. From there he made his way to Radstadt, near Salzburg, where he planned to surrender to the Americans in order to stay out of the Russians' hands, but he was captured by the American Army before he could surrender."

"And what happened to the necklace?"

"I think it's very likely that it is resting in my hand," Paul said, holding up the choker.

"And how did it come to be here?"

"Goering's house on the Obersalzberg was overrun by American troops, who sacked the place very thoroughly, drinking Goering's wines and grabbing souvenirs. I think it's likely that one of the soldiers came across the necklace and put it in his pocket. Certainly, it was never cataloged by the army. After I saw the movie *The Woman in Gold,* I did some research, and I could find no report anywhere that it ever surfaced. Spoils of war, I guess you'd say."

"Then who legally owns it?"

"Adele Bloch-Bauer died of natural causes in 1925. Her husband, Ferdinand, was her only heir. He's dead, and they had no children, and it passed to his brother-in-law, Adler. The last legal transaction regarding the necklace occurred when Adler gave it to his daughter as a wedding gift. It was taken from her by the Gestapo. She died a few years ago, in her nineties, without issue, I believe. Perhaps, in the normal course of events, it would have passed to a descendant of some distant relative. Some of her family were lost in the Holocaust, I believe, so it could be very complicated."

"What is the significance of the date, 1899, engraved in the necklace?"

"Ferdinand had the necklace made as a wedding gift for his wife, Adele. They were married in 1899."

The two men sat quietly for a long moment.

"This Fiske, mentioned in the receipt from Blume, is he Carrie Fiske's father?" Paul asked.

"Grandfather."

"Bijoux Blume was still operating in Paris in 1946. I think the last member of the family died in the late fifties or early sixties, and the business closed or was sold, perhaps to a competitor."

"Would, perhaps, whoever bought Blume still have the business records?"

"Certainly records of the Blume designs might exist. A competitor buying the business would recognize the value of keeping the drawings and records of their sales. It's all provenance, which can be key to establishing value."

"Would their designs have been photographed, as a matter of course?"

"Perhaps, particularly if the Blumes were very proud of a piece and wanted to be able to establish their connection with it. It seems likely that they would feel that way. It is — no matter who wore it or painted it or stole it — a remarkable piece of work, probably unique."

"Suppose this proved to be the original. What value would you place on it?"

"Priceless," Paul replied. "When Mrs. Adler sold *The Woman in Gold* and the other paintings, Ronald Lauder paid her a hundred and thirty-five million for them, and that was years ago. The necklace might not bring that kind of money, but in some ways, for some people, it might be an even bigger trophy, especially after the movie. There are a lot of billionaires in the world."

"Paul," Stone said, "how would you like to spend a few days in Paris, on me?"

Paul smiled. "I think I could stand that, if I can take my wife."

"You buy her ticket. I'll put you up in a suite in the Paris Arrington," Stone said. "Get your people organized for the work in the three houses, then go to Paris as soon as you're ready. Joan will arrange the hotel and your transportation."

Paul put the necklace back into its velvet pouch and dropped it into Stone's hand. "Take good care of it," he said.

"Oh, I will. And Paul, not a word of this to anyone, not even your wife."

Paul held a finger to his lips, then left.

35

Paul Eckstein went straight home and found his wife getting out of the shower. He embraced and kissed her, unmindful of her wetness.

"What was that all about?" she asked when she could take a breath. "It's been a long time since you came home at noon for a quickie."

"This isn't about a quickie," Paul replied, kissing her again. "How would you feel about a week in the best hotel in Paris?"

"Can we afford it?"

"We can, for two reasons. One, I have just been handed the biggest, most lucrative estate job of my life, and two, the job includes investigating a piece of jewelry in Paris."

"What piece of jewelry?"

"Wait right here."

"May I put some clothes on?"

"You may, if you're not interested in a

quickie." He went into his study, to the shelves where he kept a large library of art books, and came back with one on Klimt. She was still naked when he got back to the bathroom. He set the book down on the toilet seat and leafed through it to *The Woman in Gold.* "That piece," he said, pointing to the choker.

"No kidding?"

"No kidding, and remember, I didn't say a word about it. My lips are still sealed."

"What about your pointing finger?"

"That is not sealed, and it has many talents." He demonstrated one of them.

"Your finger is very talented indeed," she breathed in his ear. "Now, are we going to have our quickie in the bathtub, or shall we adjourn to the bedroom?"

They adjourned.

When they parted, breathless and perspiring, Paul said, "The beautiful thing about this assignment is that I know exactly whom to see in Paris, and it will take less than an hour to do that. The rest of the week is ours."

"I like the sound of that," she replied. "Who will you have to see?"

"A gentleman of my acquaintance who is the great-grandson of the man who designed the unmentionable piece. He is probably the last man on earth with this information in his brain."

"And who is he?"

"His name is Randol Cohn-Blume. His great-grandfather was the chief designer of Bijoux Blume, a highly respected Paris jeweler of the first half of the twentieth century. He was also the nephew of the owner. His specialty was the design and crafting of impossibly expensive jewelry for impossibly wealthy clients, and I believe him to be the designer of the unmentionable diamond-and-ruby choker."

"You couldn't just phone him?"

"Tell me, would phoning him require an all-expense-paid trip to Paris for you and me?"

"No, it would not."

"The very reason I am not already phoning him. I am advised that making phone calls from Paris to Paris is possible in this modern day and age."

"A very sensible conclusion," she replied. "When do we depart?"

"Let's see. I have to assemble three teams of catalogers and appraisers and get them to work on three very high-end residences. And after that, we can depart for Paris. Say, three days?"

"Three days it is," his wife said, getting up.

"Where are you going?" he asked. "I'm ready for another quickie."

"Nonsense. You haven't been ready that fast since you were nineteen. I have to start packing." She got out of bed, found a stepladder, and began hauling pieces of luggage from the top shelves of her dressing room. "Will we be dining out at the best restaurants in Paris every evening?" she called.

"Quite possibly," he called back.

"Oh, good, then I can take a good dress for every evening."

He got out of bed and watched his naked wife pulling things from the racks of her dressing room, assessing them and putting them back. Finally she found one acceptable and folded it carefully into her suitcase.

"I love watching you pack," he said, "especially while you're naked." He kissed her on the back of her neck.

"Now, Paul," she said, applying a firm hand to his chest. "Let's not start something we can't finish."

"It's worth a try," he said, guiding her hand downward.

"My word," she said, "you're up again."

"I certainly am," he replied, towing her

toward the bed.

"What on earth brought this on?" she asked.

"The thought of several dozen flawless diamonds and rubies," he replied, rolling on top of her.

"I should have known it wasn't me," she said, wrapping her legs around him. "Never mind, I can make do."

36

Stone and Gala met Dino and Viv for dinner at Patroon, and Bob, who had become accustomed to being treated like dog royalty by the staff, lay under the table, wrestling with a large bone.

"What are you so up about?" Dino asked.

"Isn't he often up?" Gala queried.

"Not like this, not before his first bourbon."

"Well, disposing of Carrie Fiske's estate has turned into not the drag I had expected it to be."

"Not the drag? What does that mean?"

"The opposite of a drag — interesting, even enjoyable."

"Did you discover a pot of gold under her rainbow?"

Stone and Gala exchanged a sly glance.

"Something better than a pot of gold?"

"Have you ever heard of *The Woman in Gold*?"

"The Klimt or the movie?" Dino asked.

"Either or both."

"I've seen the painting at the Neue Galerie," Dino said.

Viv piped up. "I took him by the wrist and elbow and marched him there."

"I was very happy to go," Dino said, "and we saw the movie on TV last night."

"Do you recall the necklace the woman was wearing in the painting?"

"How could I not?" Dino asked. "I wondered whatever happened to it."

"I'll enlighten you," Stone said. "It's in my safe."

"You are under arrest!" Dino said. "You could not have come by that legally."

"I found it in Carrie's jewelry safe in her New York apartment."

"The real thing?"

"It would appear to be, but that is being researched as we speak."

"Researched how?"

"I have an appraiser leaving for Paris shortly, to search for the original design drawings and, maybe, a photograph and other documentary evidence."

"Search where?"

"Among the jewelry stores of the Rue St.-Honoré, one of which may have purchased the original makers, called Bijoux Blume, which discontinued trading in the fifties or sixties."

"I want to know every detail of how it came to be in New York," Viv said.

"As far as I can tell, it was last seen adorning the neck of Frau Hermann Goering, late in World War Two. It gets very dramatic after that. Hermann burned down his country place to keep the Russians from sullying it and may have taken his wife's jewelry to their house in the Bavarian Alps, which soon after was sacked by an outfit of American soldiers."

"Band of Brothers," Dino said. "There was a scene about that in the great miniseries."

"I believe you are right, or it may have been Hitler's house."

"Of course I'm right, I've seen the thing twice."

"Did you happen to notice which soldier ended up with the diamond choker?"

"That must have happened when I wasn't looking."

"Apparently, whatever happened to the choker also happened when nobody was looking."

"What makes you think you've got the real thing?" Viv asked.

"The maker's name and the date 1899

were engraved or stamped inside. That was the year the woman received the piece as a wedding present from her husband."

"What a husband!" Viv enthused.

"Suppose it's just a copy?" Dino said.

"My appraiser says it's still worth a couple of million. I think there are more than a hundred flawless diamonds and a few dozen rubies in it."

"And what's it worth if it's real?"

"Apparently, the sky's the limit."

"Who gets the proceeds?"

"The estate, of course, and my fee is based on the value of the estate."

"Apart from this bauble, what do you think it's worth?"

"Let me put it this way. I've already been offered a hundred million for the three houses and their contents, and I think that's a lowball offer. And, of course, there's a large stock portfolio."

"How did you come to have Ms. Fiske as a client?" Viv asked.

"She came to see me because she was afraid of her ex-husband."

"We're looking for that guy now," Dino said.

"She was also anxious to get him out of her will. I went out to her East Hampton place that weekend and drew a new will, and she executed it a few days later."

"Are you mentioned in the will?" Viv asked.

"Yes, I am. I get Bob."

"Lucky you."

"Did I mention that you can't speak a word about the necklace to anybody, and I mean *anybody*?"

Everybody looked at the ceiling. "Oh, yeah, sure, got it, not a word," they murmured in chorus.

37

Stone and Gala got home fairly late, and as they walked into the master suite, the phone rang.

"Hello?"

"Good evening, Mr. Barrington."

"Well, if it isn't what's his name."

"That's unkind."

"I meant it to be. What do you want this time?"

"It was unfriendly of you to bar me from my former home. I still have my key."

"Your key now opens exactly nothing. All the locks in all three residences have been changed."

"Now, why would you do that? I desire only to collect a few of my things."

"I've had a good look around the apartment, and there isn't so much as a necktie that's yours. Carrie had it swept of your belongings and shipped them all to you."

"She neglected to ship an *objet* I gave her

as a wedding present."

"Do you not understand the word 'present,' as in gift? When you have made someone a present, it no longer belongs to you."

"It does if she doesn't want it. Carrie told me she would return the gift, but she didn't."

"Perhaps because of her untimely death," Stone pointed out.

"I tell you again, I had nothing to do with her death."

"Don't tell me, tell the police. I'm sure they'll apologize for all the bother and send you on your way with a pat on the back."

"She *said* she would return it to me."

"When was this?"

"A couple of weeks ago."

"May I remind you that she made a new will after that date that is a full and well-expressed listing of her intentions toward you and there is zero reference in it of returning anything."

"It would be much simpler for everyone if you would just return the necklace to me."

"What kind of necklace?"

"A choker of diamonds and rubies."

"And what is the provenance of this necklace?"

"It was left to me by my grandfather."

"Then, of course, you can prove that by sending me a copy of his probated will."

"I'm afraid I can't lay my hands on it, just at the moment."

"I rather thought not. And how did your grandfather acquire the necklace?"

"He obtained it while traveling in Europe many years ago."

"How many years ago?"

"Around 1945."

"I seem to recall that Europe was gripped by a widespread unpleasantness in that year. Tell me, what did your grandfather do in the war?"

"He was a sergeant in the 506th Parachute Regiment of the 101st Airborne Division."

"And where in Europe, exactly, did he obtain the necklace?"

"In southern Germany."

"Under what circumstances?"

"It was among a number of items confiscated from a private residence."

"I wonder if I can guess whose residence. Let me see, was he a large figure in the Nazi party? Am I warm?"

"You obviously know whom I am talking about."

"Obviously. Now, back to provenance. How did Herr Goering acquire the necklace?"

"My grandfather was unable to ask him, as he had already fled the premises."

"Well, let me fill you in. Goering got it from the Gestapo, who stole it, along with other belongings of certain families."

"I have heard that opinion expressed."

"Well, your grandfather should have been charged with, first, grand theft, and then with receiving stolen goods."

"Be that as it may . . ."

"So you are asking the return of stolen property that you had given to someone else?"

"That is an uncharitable view."

"Well, speaking as an attorney, I can tell you that you have no legal basis whatever for any claim on the necklace."

"It seems such a small thing to ask."

"How small? What value do you put on the necklace?"

"I concede that it is valuable."

"How valuable. Go on, tell me."

"I had it appraised once and was told it might bring a million dollars at auction."

"And who told you that?"

"An auction house."

"Which auction house?"

"It doesn't matter. Perhaps I should tell you that the necklace is a copy of the one you are thinking of."

"Is that why you whipped up that little piece of forgery about Carrie's grandfather having the necklace made in 1946?"

"I'm sure I don't know what you mean. I am not a forger."

"Well, if the document isn't a forgery, it means that Carrie's grandfather ordered the copy made in 1946, and it eventually ended up as a bequest to Carrie?"

"Well, ah . . ."

"Oh, no, that story would make a liar of you, wouldn't it? If the document wasn't a forgery, you didn't give the necklace to Carrie as a wedding present."

"Now, listen . . ."

"No, Mr. Biggers, you listen. You have burned your bridges in every possible direction. Now stop bothering me, and give yourself up to the police." Stone hung up.

"Him again?" Gala asked.

"The son of a bitch won't leave me alone."

38

On his first morning in Paris, Paul Eckstein was awakened by the doorbell in his beautiful suite at the Arrington. *"Entrez!"* he shouted, waking his wife. He pulled a sheet over her naked body as the room service waiter pushed his cart into the bedroom.

"Bonjour, M'sieur," the man said.

"Just put the table on her side of the bed," Eckstein said. "We'll serve ourselves."

The waiter did so, then departed.

"Breakfast is getting cold," he whispered in his wife's ear.

She rolled onto her back. "We're in Paris, is that right?"

"That's right."

"I wanted to be sure I wasn't dreaming." She plumped up her pillows, took the lid off a plate, and handed him his eggs Benedict. "You're going to gain weight while we're here," she said.

"I plan to," Paul replied, digging in.

She served herself, as well. "And what is your plan for today?"

"I'm going to see if I can arrange a lunch with Randol Cohn-Blume, and if so, I'm going to stop on the way at Charvet and buy a few things."

"Then perhaps I'll stop by Chanel and meet you for lunch."

"I think you'd better make your own arrangements for lunch. Randol is more talkative when fewer people are present."

"Oh, all right."

The phone rang. "With any luck that will be Randol. I left him a message last night." He picked up the phone. "Hello?"

"Paul, is that you?"

"It is, Randol. How in the world are you?"

"I'm quite well, thank you. What brings you to Paris?"

"I came in search of knowledge, and I would like to discuss that with you over lunch."

"I am available."

"Brasserie Lipp at one?" He knew that was the man's favorite restaurant.

"Lipp at one. I shall look forward to it."

"As shall I." Both men hung up.

"That sounded very cordial," Lara said.

"It was, and will remain so, as long as Randol believes himself to be well compensated for his advice."

Paul visited Charvet, selected some neckties and splurged on a cashmere dressing gown, all of which he had delivered to the Arrington. Lipp was abuzz, as usual, and Randol was already seated at his usual table. The two men shook hands, then embraced, then took their places.

"I took the liberty of ordering your wine," Randol said as the waiter poured them glasses of a chilled Meursault.

"Thank you, Randol, your grasp of enology was always better than mine." They clinked glasses and sipped.

"You're having the choucroute, of course."

"Of course."

Randol caught a waiter's eye and held up two fingers. "You're looking very well, Paul, prosperous, even."

"I can't complain — well, I could complain, but it wouldn't do any good." The two men laughed at the little joke.

"And what knowledge do you seek in Paris?"

Paul decided to be oblique; it might save him money in the end. "Tell me," he said, "was your father still working in 1946?"

"Indeed, yes. He worked until 1959, when the firm was acquired, and then for another five years under the new management."

"Was he engaged in original work, still, or mostly in copying his old designs?"

"Both, I should imagine. Pickings had been lean during the war years, of course, except for pieces ordered by the Germans. What interests you about that period?"

"A client of mine, a prominent New York attorney, is the executor of a rather interesting estate, and he has engaged me to appraise the jewelry, among other things."

"I see. Are there some pieces from Blume included?"

"Only one. It comes with a receipt from 1946, for a copy of a piece designed in 1899."

"Ah, that would be near the beginning of my father's long career. He would have been working under his uncle, François, at that time. What was the piece, and who ordered it?"

"It was a diamond-and-ruby choker, ordered by a Viennese, Ferdinand Bloch-Bauer, as a wedding gift for his wife."

"Ah, of course, the piece in the Klimt painting. A great loss, that."

"Loss? How so?"

"Well, it disappeared around the end of the war. Hermann Goering had appropriated it, and it never turned up after he was arrested by the Allies."

"Yes, that is sad. The receipt mentions that the copy was made from the original designs. Do those still exist?"

"Well, as you know, Blume was acquired by Aubergonois et Fis, in 1964. Most of the value of their purchase, apart from some loose stones, was in the Blume designs."

Paul's heart leapt. "Are they still in business?"

"No, they went under in '89."

Paul's heart sank. "Ah. Any idea what happened to the designs?"

"I could investigate that for you. They could have ended up in an incinerator."

"Well, if you have the time, my client would be happy to see them."

"Merely to view, or to purchase?"

"I imagine that copies would do, but I can inquire if he has any interest in the originals. He did ask about the possibility of a photograph of the original, so that he could compare his copy and have some judgment made about the quality of the workmanship in the estate piece."

"And who would make that judgment, Paul?" Randol asked archly.

"I believe I would be asked to cast an eye over it."

"I rather thought so."

Their choucroute arrived, and their talk turned to other things. When they parted, Randol promised to phone in a day or two.

Back at the Arrington, Paul swept into the suite, to find his wife gazing at herself in the mirror, wearing a Chanel suit with a tag still on it.

"You look happy."

"It was a productive lunch."

"Did your friend have the information you want?"

"Oh, he wouldn't tell me if he did, he wants to use the suspense to get his price up. But if anyone can find it, he can, believe me." He checked out the Chanel. "Buy another, if you like."

39

Stone was a little later than usual getting to his desk; Gala's early-morning demands had detained him. He got off the elevator and walked into his office. Bob was entertaining a visitor, someone Stone knew he should know, but he could not, for the life of him, come up with a name.

"Good morning," he said, shaking the man's hand. "Will you excuse me for just a moment? Can I get you some coffee?"

"Of course, and of course," the man said. He appeared to be in his early fifties, gray-haired, finely tailored.

"I'll be right back." Stone closed the door behind him and went into Joan's office. "Who is that on my sofa?"

"Bob? You know how he loves that sofa."

"The man, not the dog."

"I'm sorry, I just got in. Fred must have let him in."

"He wants coffee. Figure it out."

Stone sat down at Joan's desk and slapped his forehead. *Who is that guy?* he asked himself.

Joan returned. It's Barnaby Cabot."

"Any relation to Lance Cabot?"

"Probably. He's the attorney general."

"Of New York?"

"Of the United States."

Stone slapped himself again. *"Oh, shit!"* He got up and ran for the door. "Sorry about that. How are you, sir?"

"Barney, please. I know we haven't met, but I prefer informality."

"As you wish." Stone sat down. "You and Bob seem to be getting on well."

"Oh, yes, Labs are my favorites. I grew up with them. I believe we're neighbors in Dark Harbor."

Stone had a house there, on the island of Islesboro, in Maine.

"I don't think I knew that."

"Oh, we live quietly when we're there — a little sailing, a little golf, that's about it."

"Same for me." Stone was waiting to be told why the attorney general of the United States was sitting in his office, unannounced.

"I was in the city, and I thought I'd drop by," Cabot said.

"I'm delighted to see you," Stone managed to say. He was missing something: Had the man called or written to him? If so, why couldn't he remember that? Was this what dementia was like?

"Excellent coffee. What is it?"

"Medaglia d'Oro, an Italian espresso roast."

"Where can I find it?"

"Joan will send you some."

"Thanks, I'd like that. Justice Department coffee is dreadful stuff."

"I'll bet."

Silence ensued. Finally, Stone couldn't stand it anymore. "Barney, to what do I owe the pleasure?"

"Oh, that. Kate asked me to speak to you."

"Oh, good." Kate, the President? Kate Smith? Kate Blanchett? No, that one was with a C. "How is Kate?"

"Thriving. I've never seen anybody enjoy that office so much."

Ah, Kate the President of the United States. "What can I do for her — and you?"

"She has asked me to put together a small ad hoc committee — a very confidential committee — to meet three or four candidates for the Court and give her our assessments."

"The *Supreme* Court?"

"That one, yes."

"I didn't get to the *Times* this morning — did someone die?"

"Not yet."

That stopped Stone in his tracks. A little joke seemed a good idea: "Is someone finally going to shoot one of them?"

That turned out to be a better joke than Stone had intended. Cabot doubled over with laughter, and it took him a moment to get control of himself. He wiped away tears. "Not that I know of, but I'd volunteer!" He doubled over again at his own joke.

I know what it is, Stone thought. I'm still asleep, and this is a bizarre dream.

Cabot took a deep breath and got ahold of himself. "There's a rumor, I take it, that someone is going to resign. I don't know who, but Kate, apparently, takes it seriously, and she wants to get a jump on the process. I've put together a group of four, and I'm not supposed to tell any of you who else is involved. Kate wants us to meet three people, individually, and talk with her about each of them — nothing in writing. Two of them are women."

"Oh?"

"And one is a gay man."

"Am I allowed to know their names?"

"They are Congressman Terrence Maher, Senator Marisa Bond, and the United States attorney for the Southern District of New York, Tiffany Baldwin."

Stone hoped he didn't wince at the mention of Tiffany's name. He had had a fling with the woman some years ago, and she periodically tried to relight the flame. He was terrified of her.

"Do you know any of them?"

"I know Maher and Bond from their television appearances, but I haven't met them. I'm acquainted with Baldwin."

"And?"

"And I avoid her, when possible."

"You don't get along, then?"

"I don't see her often enough for that to come up."

"Ah."

Yes, Ah.

Cabot rummaged in his briefcase and came up with three files. "Here is background on each of them. It's quite thorough and contains some materials from FBI files, so the files are, of course, quite confidential. Each of the candidates will call your office and make an appointment."

Cabot hadn't inquired if Stone would do it; he had, rightly, assumed that any friend of Kate Lee would help if he could.

"Well, my car is waiting," Cabot said, getting to his feet and disturbing Bob, whose head was in his lap.

"Joan will brush you off," Stone said. "She's used to it."

"Thank you for seeing me." The two men shook hands.

"Kate will call you in a week or so to hear your impressions."

"I'll look forward to speaking with her."

The man left, and Stone buzzed Joan. "Three people are going to call for appointments: Congressman Terrence Maher, Senator Marisa Bond, and fucking Tiffany Baldwin."

Joan burst out laughing.

"I'll see the first two here or wherever they like in the city. I'll meet Tiffany somewhere cozy, like the middle of Grand Central Station. I do not, repeat *not,* wish to be alone in any room with her."

"Got it, boss."

"And send the attorney general a dozen cans of Medaglia d'Oro."

"Right."

40

Paul Eckstein woke on his fourth day in Paris and stared at the ceiling. He had not heard a word from Randol Cohn-Blume.

"How long has it been?" his wife asked. They were waiting for breakfast.

"Four days."

"Is he usually this slow?"

"I think he's dragging it out in the hope of more money."

"How much did you offer him?"

"I didn't make an offer. I'm waiting for him to tell me what he wants."

The doorbell rang, and Paul shouted, *"Entrez!"*

The waiter came in, knowing by now where to put the table. He left them to it.

"Well," she said, "I'm certainly enjoying our visit, but you're not."

"Of course I am."

"You're wound too tight to enjoy yourself."

"Nonsense." The phone rang, and he levitated about a foot.

"Perfectly relaxed, eh?"

Paul took a deep breath. "Hello?"

"Paul, it is Randol."

"Good morning, Randol."

"I hope I am not calling too early."

"No, we're just having breakfast."

"Can we meet in an hour?"

"Can you make it two hours? We're slow starters." He didn't want to seem too anxious.

"All right, an hour and a half, then." He gave Paul an address in the Rue St.-Honoré. "It's just a doorway — we'll meet outside."

"All right, an hour and a half." Paul hung up.

"Feeling better now?" his wife asked.

"A little. I mean, if he didn't have anything, he'd have told me so on the phone."

"It's Valentino for me, today, then Saint Laurent."

Paul got out of a taxi and found Randol waiting beside a door in a blank wall.

"Ah, there you are." Randol produced a key, unlocked the door, and they went inside, where Randol locked it behind him. He handed Paul a small, heavy flashlight. "We don't want to turn on any lights down here. It would set off the alarm system."

"Are we breaking and entering?" Paul asked, trying his flashlight. It was extremely powerful, in spite of its small size.

"In a manner of speaking," Randol replied. "Follow me." He started down a winding staircase that went on longer than Paul had expected. At the bottom, Randol followed a hallway until he came to a door, which he unlocked with another key, then locked behind them. "There," he said, playing his light along a wall before them. It was covered with steel shelving, cabinets, and file drawers.

"Where?" Paul asked.

"That is for us to find out. We will start at opposite ends and work toward the center. Your French is good enough to read this stuff, isn't it?"

"As long as it's typed. I have trouble reading the handwriting of Frenchmen."

"If it is in longhand, you will find it very neat and correct. How do you say . . . boilerplate?"

"That's not the word, but I know what you mean." Paul went to his end and turned on his light. "What are we looking for?"

"The name Blume, and the years 1899 and 1946. If you find those, let me know."

Nearly four hours later, Paul's back hurt, he was painfully hungry, and he had covered only about a third of the distance to the middle of the wall. Then he read a tab saying: *Blume, 1894.* "Randol, I think I may have something here."

Randol joined him and looked at the file. "Excellent," he said. "Let's both keep going here." The two men pawed through the files, some of them thick, until they came to 1899. "Ah," Randol said, "success."

There were more than a dozen files labeled with that year, and one of them read *Bloch-Bauer.* It was a thick accordion file. Randol took it to a steel table in the center of the room and unwound the cord sealing it.

Paul's heart was thudding against his rib cage. He watched as Randol examined each page, then came to a folded sheet of heavier paper. "Oh, yes," he said, unfolding the sheet to its full size, about one foot by two and a half. On the sheet, finely rendered in India ink, were four drawings of the choker, each from a different angle, with each stone delineated, and the rubies colored in. On the lower right-hand corner of the sheet was the signature *François Blume, mai 1899.*

"I believe the expression is 'pay dirt,' " Randol said.

"I believe you are right. Are there photographs of the finished piece?"

"Not in this file," Randol said. He returned to the file drawer and brought out another file of a different, heavier paper. He opened it and withdrew a packet of soft paper, which, when opened, had four compartments. Randol removed a pair of white cotton gloves from a pocket, put them on, then withdrew from the file a glass negative of about eight by ten inches. He played the light over the sheet, then removed and examined four more negatives. "Each is of the necklace from the angles depicted in the drawing," he said, "except for this one." The final negative was a photograph of the inside of the necklace.

Paul pointed at some small lettering and shone his light on it. "Can you make out what this says?"

Randol produced a loupe and held it gently against the glass. "It says, 'Bijoux Blume 1899.' "

Paul sucked in a breath. "Can we get copies of these?" he asked.

Randol gave a short laugh. "Why don't we just steal them?"

41

Paul ordered his lunch, then excused himself; in the men's room he called Stone Barrington.

"Paul?"

"It's me, Stone."

"How's it going?"

"As well as I had hoped. We found the original designs."

"That's wonderful."

"Now I need five thousand euros in cash, and I didn't bring that much. It's for the man who led me to the drawings, and it's worth every cent."

"I'll call the Arrington and have them give you the cash, then charge my account."

"Thank you, Stone."

"When will you be back in New York?"

"In a day or two."

"Take the weekend. I'll see you Monday." Stone hung up. Paul used the men's room, then went back to the table, which was at a small restaurant across the street from the photographer who was doing the work. He sat down, and his lunch arrived. "Your cash will be available at my hotel when we're done," he said.

"I believe we are done," Randol said. "All we have to do is collect the prints that are being made as we speak."

"No, we're not done. We have to go back to the archive and search 1946 to see if Blume made a copy of the necklace, then we have to replace the original designs and glass negatives."

"That's unnecessary, I assure you."

"Randol, what if someone wants to check the authenticity of our prints? What if the originals are needed for that?"

"I could retain them."

"They don't belong to you."

"A small point."

"A very important point. The originals must be put back into the files where we found them."

"Oh, all right."

They finished their lunch in silence, then crossed the street to the photographer's. Paul examined the copies of the designs and the prints from the glass negatives and pronounced himself satisfied. The photographer handed them over in a stout folder and accepted payment.

Twenty minutes later they were back in the archive room, replacing the designs and negatives in their original wrappings and in their original places.

"Now, for 1946," he said.

Both of them riffled through the drawers and located the date. They went through every piece of paper and found no reference to Blume's having copied the necklace.

"That's it," Paul said. "Let's lock up and get out of here."

They did so and took a cab to the Arrington, where Paul called at the front desk and found a thick envelope waiting for him. He handed it to Randol. "There you are, my friend, not a bad day's work, eh?"

"Not bad."

"Be sure to return that key to its lawful owner," Paul said. "And please understand, it may be necessary to find the originals we copied, and if they are not there, the police will be looking for you."

"Paul, you offend me."

"I don't intend to, just to impress upon you the importance of acting properly in this case."

"I understand." They embraced, kissed on

both cheeks, and Randol disappeared into a cab.

Paul went upstairs to see his wife.

"Is it done?" she asked.

"It is done. And mark my words, when we get back, all hell is going to break loose."

On Monday morning Stone greeted Paul in his office. "You look jet-lagged," he said.

"And I feel jet-lagged." He placed a large envelope on Stone's desk and explained what he had found in Paris.

Stone removed the contents of the envelope and looked at the prints, then he went to his safe and brought back the necklace. "Let's compare it to the photographs," he said, shaking the choker into his hand. He laid the choker facedown on his desk and set the photograph next to it, then handed Paul a magnifying glass. "You first."

Paul went carefully over the photos. "First, the name and date are in exactly the same place," he said. "In fact, every detail of your necklace is identical to the photograph. Stone, you have the original Adele Bloch-Bauer necklace. There is no disputing it. The original drawings and plates have been returned to the archive, and if there is ever any doubt cast on the authenticity of this piece, they are there for inspection."

"What about 1946?"

"Blume made no copy of the necklace in that year, and we checked 1945 and 1947, too. If they had made a copy, it would have been in the file."

Stone sat down, took a deep breath, and let it out. "Now what?" he said, half to himself.

"I gave this a great deal of thought on the way home," Paul said. "Will you need to sell the necklace for the benefit of the estate?"

"Yes, I suppose so. I'm obligated to get the most for it that I can."

"Do you have any discretion in the disposition of the estate?"

"To a degree. There is a list of organizations and charities that will benefit."

"May I make a suggestion?"

"Of course."

"When the news breaks of the existence of this necklace, it is going to become the most famous piece of jewelry in the world, at least for a time. When that happens, people, perhaps distant relatives of the former owner, might well appear to claim it."

"That had occurred to me."

"Do any of the organizations mentioned in the will have a Jewish orientation?"

"Yes, the Holocaust Museum, in Washington."

"You might think of making that museum the beneficiary of the auction."

"That's a brilliant idea," Stone said. "It would certainly simplify my life."

"Are you acquainted with anyone at the big auction houses?"

"I know Jamie Niven, at Sotheby's."

"You might ask him to conduct the auction and waive the house's fees in favor of the museum. They would get an enormous amount of publicity from the sale."

"I'll call Jamie today."

"Sotheby's would organize a publicity campaign around the sale, in order to drum up bidders. Be sure you have all your ducks in a row before you make this public. You don't want to be overwhelmed."

"Paul, I can't thank you enough for that advice."

"Now, as to the rest of the estate. In a week or so we will have completed our cataloging and appraisal of the three residences, and I'll give you a written report. At that time, we can talk about what you might want to sell for the estate and what you might include in the sale of the houses. In the meantime, you might want to be sure that everything is insured."

"I've already done that — Steele is the insurer, and I sit on their board. The necklace is insured for a million dollars, but in light of what you discovered in Paris, perhaps I should increase that. What value should I put on the necklace?"

"I should think ten million dollars."

"I'll do that today."

The two men shook hands; Paul left, and Stone returned the necklace to his safe.

42

Stone sat in a comfortable chair in the office of Jamie Niven, the chairman of Sotheby's. He took him through the history of the past few weeks, and showed him the photographs of the designs and the necklace.

"Where is the necklace now? Do you have access to it?" Niven asked.

Stone took the velvet bag from his pocket and shook out the choker into Niven's hand.

"Good God," Niven said, examining the piece carefully. "Excuse me for a moment." He went to his desk, picked up a phone, and issued some orders, then hung up. "Come with me, Stone." He walked next door to a conference room, where someone was setting up a microscope. He handed a woman the drawings and the necklace.

She looked at the designs with a magnifying glass. "These look good," she said. "They are typical of Blume's work at the turn of the last century. I've no reason to doubt their authenticity."

"The originals are available in Paris," Stone said, "if they need to be seen."

"Let's hear from Pierre," Niven said, nodding toward the man at the microscope, who was inspecting the necklace under it, while consulting the photographs. "The stones are genuine — top quality in both the diamonds and the rubies. The piece is a perfect representation of the designs and photographs."

"It's not a copy?" Niven asked.

"In my opinion, it is undoubtedly the original."

Stone took an envelope from his pocket and handed it to Niven. "I found this in Carrie Fiske's jewelry safe," he said. "I believe the piece was stolen when the U.S. Army ransacked Hermann Goering's alpine retreat in 1945, and the grandson of the soldier who stole it had that letter, ostensibly from Blume, forged when he gave the piece to Carrie Fiske as a wedding gift. The people who found the designs and photographs in the Paris archive also searched the years 1945, 1946, and 1947. They found no reference to Blume having copied the necklace."

"Who searched the archive for you?"

Niven asked.

"Paul Eckstein and Randol Cohn-Blume, the great-grandson of the designer François Blume."

"Paul is a good man," Niven said. "Does anybody have the slightest doubt that this piece is the original as depicted in the drawings and photographs?" His two colleagues shook their heads.

"Then that settles it for me. Stone, let's go back to my office."

When they were settled, Niven said, "How can we help?"

"I'd like you to auction the necklace, with the proceeds to go to the National Holocaust Museum, in Washington, D.C., and to waive your fees."

"We have a fifteen percent buyer's fee that we'd need to collect. Our expenses will be considerable."

"That's reasonable. I will be selecting items from the estate — American antique furniture, artwork, and jewelry for sale. By way of thanks, I'll assign those to Sotheby's at your usual rates."

"Thank you, we accept. When would you like to sell the necklace?"

"As soon as planning and publicity will allow," Stone said.

"I'd like you to leave the necklace with

us," Niven said, "for cleaning and any necessary repairs, which, I assure you, will be carried out with the greatest care."

"Then I'll need a receipt, of course, with a value of ten million."

"Of course. Is the piece insured?"

"Yes, for that amount."

"Good." Niven took a sheet of stationery from his desk, handwrote a receipt, and handed it to Stone. "Good enough?"

"Good enough."

"Did you have any security with you when you came here?"

"No."

"It was just in your pocket?"

"Yes."

"Stone, I am appalled. This necklace should never be alone with anyone again."

"I'm glad it will be in your safe, not mine. One more thing, Jamie."

"Yes?"

"I will be a bidder for the piece."

"Personally, or for someone else?"

"Personally, and I would like my interest held in the strictest confidence."

Niven turned to his computer, typed a few keystrokes, then printed out a sheet and handed it to Stone. "You now have a numbered buyer's account with us," he said. "When you speak to your bidder, or anyone else here, give your number, not your name, and your identity will be known only to me."

The two men shook hands. "I'll speak to my people, and we'll come up with a sale date."

Stone elected to walk home, feeling lighter than before, now that the necklace was in the safekeeping of someone else.

43

Stone helped Fred get Gala's luggage into the Bentley, then took her in his arms. "I'm sorry you have to leave," he said.

"I've had a wonderful time, but my screenplay is finished, and now I have to do some revisions and attend some production meetings in L.A."

"I understand, I just don't like it."

"I want you to think of yourself as having a house in Santa Fe," she said. "I'll share anytime you can come."

"What a wonderful offer! I'll take you up on it."

She kissed him, got into the Bentley, and was driven away by Fred.

Stone went back to his office. Paul Eckstein was due any minute with his report on the Fiske real estate. He looked at his watch, and as he did, Joan buzzed.

"Paul Eckstein is here."

"Send him in."

Paul entered Stone's office and placed three leather-bound albums on his desk. "Here we are," he said. "Shall I go over them with you?"

"Please."

Paul took him through each of the three albums, showing him photographs of all the rooms of each house, along with shots of furniture and art that had been individually appraised. Paul handed him a bound report. "Here is the detail that supports the photographs. I think you'll want to read it carefully in your own time, but I'll give you the short version."

"Please do."

"We appraised the New York apartment at fifty million dollars. The Palm Beach house came in at thirty-six million, and the East Hampton house at thirty million, for a total of a hundred and sixteen million dollars, without the separately appraised pieces of art, of course." He handed Stone some sheets of paper. "Here is a list of the pieces of furniture and art, keyed to the photographs in the albums, each with a range of predicted sale prices. At the mid-range sale price, the art and furniture from both houses and the New York apartment are valued at another thirty-six million dollars. That gives you a total value of the estate of a hundred and fifty-two million dollars. Again, that's a mid-range valuation of both the real estate and the art."

"I've had an offer of a hundred million for the three residences," Stone said, "without some of the art."

"That's low, I believe. As for the furniture and art, some of it could go at lowball prices, while other pieces might attract competition at an auction and bring top dollar. Ms. Fiske's jewelry and clothing are not included. There's a separate sheet for what those might bring. There are some ball gowns and haute couture dresses that the Metropolitan Museum might like to have for their costume collection, if you want to donate them. Or they might bring a couple of hundred thousand dollars at auction."

"How much is her jewelry worth?"

"Without the Bloch-Bauer necklace, around eight million dollars, sold at auction. Again, that's a mid-level price."

"This is very fine work, Paul," Stone said. "Send me your bill."

Paul took an envelope from his pocket and handed it to Stone. "Here you are."

Stone opened the envelope and looked at the bill. "This is acceptable. I'll have Joan write you a check on the estate account." He buzzed her and gave her the instructions. She brought the check in to be signed.

"I have one more thing for you," Paul said, "a little surprise."

"I love a surprise."

Paul opened the larger of his two briefcases and took out a handsome box.

"What is it?"

"It's the Blume box that the necklace was delivered in." He opened it. "We found it in the closet, near the jewelry safe. It's rosewood, lined in velvet, a tiny bit worse for the wear, but quite beautiful, don't you think?"

"I do."

"And it has a plate on the bottom with the Blume name and the date 1899."

"The perfect companion to the piece. Sotheby's will be thrilled."

The two men shook hands, and Paul took his leave.

Stone called Nicky Chalmers, told him that the estate appraisals were in and that they should meet to discuss the matter.

Nicky and Vanessa came in that afternoon, and Stone went over the appraisals with them. "The estate makes you this offer," he said. "You may purchase the three residences for a hundred and sixteen million dollars, furnished, with the exception of these pieces." He held up the document. "You may purchase any of the pieces of furniture and art on the auction list at the projected mid-range price. I'll leave you to look over the list."

Stone left them alone in his study for half an hour, then returned.

"All right," Nicky said. "We will buy the residences for a hundred and sixteen million, and I've checked the pieces of furniture and art we'd like to purchase, as well." He handed Stone a sheet of paper. "We make the total eleven million dollars for the furniture and art, a hundred and twenty-seven million total."

"Excellent," Stone said.

"Shall I write you a check?"

Stone laughed. "I'll draw up a contract, you can have your attorney go over it, and when you're ready, we'll close the deal."

"Stone," Nicky said, "you are our attorney."

"I'm afraid I can't represent both sides in the sale. I can recommend an attorney, if you like, or you can choose someone to read the contract for you."

"I'll call you with a name," Nicky said.

Stone stood up to see them out. "I can have the contract for you in a few days, then take whatever time you need to have an attorney review it, and we'll make a date for the closing. By the way, I heard from Harvey again. He's trying to claim a piece of jewelry that wasn't on the list you saw — says he gave it to Carrie as a wedding gift."

"That would make it hers, not his, wouldn't it?"

"Exactly what I told him. Nicky, will you tell me again about seeing Harvey in Santa Fe?"

"Well, we ran into some acquaintances — Derek and Alicia Bedford, you met them in East Hampton."

"I remember them."

"Well, we bumped into them in the plaza and adjourned to the Inn of the Anasazi for lunch. That's right off the plaza, across the street from the old governor's mansion. As we left the hotel, we walked across the plaza to their car, and on the way we saw Harvey looking at the Indian jewelry under the portico of the mansion."

"Did the Bedfords know Harvey?"

"They had met him once or twice, I think."

"Would they testify to seeing him there?"

"I expect so."

"After Harvey is caught, the DA might want to interview them."

"If I run into them again, I'll tell them.

Why don't I write down their number for you?"

Stone gave him paper and pen, and he wrote down the information.

"Thank you, Nicky." They left, and Stone called Jamie Niven. "How are the plans for the sale going, Jamie?"

"I've got a date for you, Stone — six weeks from today, if that's convenient for you."

"It is," Stone replied, marking it on his calendar. "Now, I have some fine pieces of furniture and art for your people to look at, mostly in New York, but a dozen pieces in Palm Beach, as well as a hundred or so pieces of jewelry."

"I think we should bring the Palm Beach pieces here, and have one big sale with everything in it, and the necklace at the very end. We'll get a huge attendance. The publicity campaign is starting immediately."

"Sounds good."

"I'll send some people to Palm Beach tomorrow, and let's make a date for my team to see what's in New York."

"Any day this week."

"Tomorrow at nine AM?"

"Let's make it ten AM."

"We'll see you there."

Half an hour later Joan came into his office.

252

"That Biggers guy is on the phone again."

"Call Dino and get a trace started." Stone picked up the phone. "All right, what is it this time?"

"I understand that you're going to sell my necklace at auction," Biggers said.

"You're very well informed, except about the ownership of the necklace."

"That sale will never happen," Biggers said.

"It will, and you can't do anything to stop it."

"Mark my words, Mr. Barrington, your sale will blow up in your face." He hung up.

Stone buzzed Joan. "Never mind the trace, just get me Dino."

"Bacchetti."

"Biggers is still calling me. I couldn't keep him on long enough for a trace. The guy is very savvy about that."

"Leave it to me," Dino said.

44

Stone met Jamie Niven and his people at Carrie Fiske's apartment the following morning. The Sotheby's people were very impressed.

"I'd like to sell the entire contents," Jamie said.

"I'm afraid I sold all three of her houses yesterday, and most of the art and furnishings." He gave Niven a listing of the others. "Here's a list of the unsold pieces, with photographs. You can add them to your auction."

"Right. I've got people at the Palm Beach house right now," Jamie said, "and we'll get to the East Hampton property tomorrow."

They went into Carrie's dressing room, and Stone opened the safe for Niven and his jewelry appraiser.

"This is quite a collection," Jamie said.

"It's three generations' worth," Stone pointed out. "Why don't you have a look through the clothes, as well — you might want to include some of the things in the auction with the jewelry."

"We'll do that. My people are going to be here most of the day," Jamie said.

"And here's something nice." He gave him the box for the necklace.

"We'll touch it up a bit and display the necklace in it."

Stone gave him keys to the properties. "The Hockneys and a Modigliani went to the buyer," he said. "Lock up here when you're finished."

"I'll bring you the key and a receipt for whatever we take with us."

"Good enough."

Stone went back to his office and entered through the street door.

"Another unannounced Cabot," Joan said.

Stone went into his office and found Lance Cabot stretched out on his sofa, sipping coffee and reading the *Times*.

"Good morning, Stone," Lance drawled. Lance seemed always to drawl. He had succeeded Kate Lee as director of Central Intelligence.

"Mind if I sit down?" Stone asked.

"Oh, shut up."

"To what do I owe the pleasure, Lance?"

"You're interfering with one of my people,

and I thought we should have a chat about it."

"I haven't spoken to any of your people recently," Stone said. He was under contract to the CIA as a consultant, though he still wasn't sure what that meant.

"I'm referring to Harvey Biggers," Lance said.

Stone sank into his chair. "What on earth are you talking about?"

"I'm not surprised that you're surprised," Lance said. "You weren't meant to know — even his wife didn't know."

"Do you understand that the police are looking for him? That he's a suspect in the murder of his ex-wife?"

"That's a load of horseshit, Stone, and the police are not looking for him. I had a word with Dino and with that bumpkin from East Hampton. If you knew Harvey, you'd know that he would never have killed her."

"I know no such thing."

"Please cite for me the evidence of his guilt."

"He was seen in Santa Fe the day before she was murdered, fifty miles away."

"So what?"

"He threatened Carrie."

"That's *her* story. Lots of women feel

threatened by their ex-husbands."

"Then he came here and told me that *she* was trying to kill *him,* not the other way around."

"Oh, that story was just a little tradecraft. Harvey probably thought it would throw you off his scent. He's always had more imagination than was good for him."

"I thought Harvey was something in finance, not a CIA officer."

"He used that as a cover — so did Holly Barker, when she had to reveal all to a co-op board to buy her apartment. We established the firm twenty-odd years ago, and it's entirely fake. Harvey is a career officer. We recruited him right out of Yale. He was Holly's operational deputy in the New York station, before she went to the National Security Council."

"Well, all that is wonderful, but how do you know Harvey didn't kill his wife?"

"Because, on the afternoon of the day Harvey was spotted by your friends in Santa Fe, he boarded an airplane for D.C."

"And how do you know he was on that airplane?"

"I know, because I sent the plane for him. He was needed at the interrogation of a former asset of his. And he arrived on time. The Agency is the family business for Harvey — his grandfather was OSS, then CIA."

"Tell me about the grandfather," Stone said.

"Ah, Henry Biggers, what a character! Henry was an associate in Bill Donovan's law firm. When Roosevelt decided we needed an intelligence agency during the war, he appointed Wild Bill to run it, and Bill pretty much staffed it out of his own address book. Henry had some language skills, and he was sent, first to London to learn what the Brits knew, then into France as an agent. He roamed far and wide, doing pretty much whatever he wanted to, and he was very productive."

"Was he ever a paratrooper? Harvey told me he was."

"That's nonsense. Henry told people whatever they wanted to hear — this was at the end of the war, when he was running around in various military disguises, chasing Nazis."

"Did he have anything to do with capturing Goering?"

"No, he was too late. He got to Goering's house on the Obersalzberg less than an hour after Hermann had fled. When the first American troops arrived at the house they found Henry Biggers sitting in the dining room, wearing the uniform of an army colonel, eating a large steak, and washing it down with — legend has it — a Lafite '29 from Goering's cellar. Shortly after that, he drove away in one of Hermann's cars, a nifty Mercedes Roadster, with several pieces of Louis Vuitton luggage strapped to it, allegedly containing various valuables from the house and quite a lot of Swiss francs."

"Was one of those pieces of luggage Frau Goering's jewelry box?"

"Indeed, it was. Henry motored down to the Swiss border, changing clothes along the way, and passed himself off as an American diplomat, which wasn't difficult, since he had a diplomatic passport, among several pieces of identification, all of them in different names."

"How'd he get the car into Switzerland?"

"Oh, he had a nicely forged bill of sale for it, on Goering's personal letterhead. Anyway, he looked up his pal Allen Dulles, who was OSS station chief in Bern, and moved into his place for a few days, while he got things squared away. He sold several loose stones from Frau Goering's collection, bought a lakeside villa, and with Allen's help, secured a Swiss passport and opened an account in a rather elegant private bank, where he deposited his cash and put the jewelry box in the vault. Word was, that he put Harvey through Yale with the proceeds from that box.

"He worked for Allen until Dulles was sent to Berlin, then discharged himself from the OSS and lived the life of Riley in Bern, until Dulles summoned him home to help out at the Agency in 1950, after Beetle Smith took over as director."

"All right, then, if Harvey didn't murder Carrie, who did?"

"Someone else, I expect. That's for you and that county sheriff in New Mexico to figure out."

"Lance, tell Harvey for me that the necklace his grandfather lifted from Goering's house is being sold at Sotheby's next month, for the benefit of the Holocaust Museum in Washington, and there's not a goddamned thing he can do about it, and to stop calling me."

"I'll pass that on, dear boy," Lance drawled, then excused himself and left, taking Stone's *Times* with him.

45

Stone called Dino.

"Bacchetti."

"I understand you and Lance Cabot are in bed together these days."

"Don't tell Viv, she'll be jealous."

"Why didn't you tell me that Harvey Biggers was no longer a suspect? You're keeping secrets from *me*?"

"Jesus, Stone, we're not married. Didn't you know that?"

"Don't evade the issue."

"What's the issue?"

"I've been running around thinking I have to capture Harvey Biggers if I get a chance."

"Well, I'm happy to tell you that you don't have to do that anymore."

"How long has this been going on?"

"How long has what been going on?"

"You and Lance and Harvey Biggers."

"We're not having a threesome."

"How long?"

"I don't remember, exactly."

"Now you're being evasive."

"I'm a public official, I have a constitutional right to be evasive."

"Okay — now who's the chief suspect in Carrie Fiske's murder?"

"I'm told there was a couple in Santa Fe who might have been involved, but I don't know their names yet."

"Hang on a minute." Stone rummaged around his desk until he found the piece of paper Nicky Chalmers had given him. "How about Derek and Alicia Bedford?"

"Who's that?"

"The couple who were in Santa Fe when Carrie was murdered."

"How do we know we're talking about the same couple?"

"Well, at least I've got names — what have you got?"

"Just Harvey's contention that he saw this couple in the plaza. Who are Derek and Alicia Bedford?"

"They're a couple I met at Carrie's house in East Hampton."

"And why do you think they may have murdered Carrie?"

"Why does Harvey think so?"

"He thinks they're sneaky people."

"Sneaky? Is that a motive for murder these days?"

"Harvey thinks so. He thinks they murdered her to get that necklace you're selling at Sotheby's."

"How did you know it's being sold at Sotheby's?"

"I read it an hour ago on Page Six of the *Post,* not that I read Page Six of the *Post.*"

"You know you do."

"I saw it by accident, as I was turning to the sports pages."

"Well, Jamie Niven is moving faster than I thought."

"Sotheby's is good at publicity for their sales. Hang on a second, I want to run these two names you gave me."

"I'm hanging." He could hear keyboard clicks from the other end.

"Okay, I ran them — they don't exist."

"What do you mean they don't exist? I met them."

"Well, they don't exist under those names."

"I've got a phone number for them."

"Give it to me."

Stone read it out.

"That's a throwaway phone," Dino said.

"Well, maybe they haven't thrown it away, yet."

"You want me to call them?"

"If they're suspects, I want you to catch them. Do a search on the phone."

"Hang on."

"Hanging."

More clicking of keys. "I got a ping at what seems to be the Carlyle Hotel."

"Go get 'em."

"I'll send somebody over there and see if we can find them. They might be just having lunch."

"If so, interrupt them. I'll get my sheriff buddy in Rio Arriba County to check out the hotels in Santa Fe."

"Lots of hotels in Santa Fe."

"All right, then the ones near the plaza."

"Okay, you do your thing, and I'll do mine."

"Oh, Dino?"

"Yeah?"

"How do I get in touch with Harvey?"

"He's back at his apartment. I'll give you the number." He did. "Why do you want to get in touch with him? I thought you never wanted to speak to him again."

"Who knows? I may want to apologize to him for thinking he was a murderer, when he's only a CIA agent."

"Lance told you that?"

"He did. Harvey is a career man, joined

right out of Yale."

"I thought that was a secret."

"Well, he told you, didn't he?" Stone hung up.

46

Stone Googled the Rio Arriba County Sheriff's Office and called the number.

"Sheriff's Office."

"May I speak to Sheriff Martinez, please?"

"Who's calling?"

"Stone Barrington."

"One moment." A pause, then, "Mr. Barrington?"

"Yes, how are you, Sheriff?"

"Call me Ray."

"And I'm Stone."

"I'm real good. You?"

"Good. Tell me, have you made any progress on the Carrie Fiske murder?"

"Well, that's a real embarrassing question, and I'm afraid the answer is embarrassing, too. It's no. I got a call from somebody in Washington, D.C., alibiing that fella, what's his name, Biggert?"

"Biggers, Harvey."

"That's the one. Well, I got this call saying

that Biggers was in New York at the time of the murder, and the guy wrote me a letter, too. First time I ever got a letter from the CIA. I had it framed."

"No other suspects, then?"

"Nope, not a single one."

"I've got two for you."

"I'm real glad to hear that. Who are they?"

"A couple, Derek and Alicia Bedford." He spelled the names.

"They live around here?"

"No, and where they live is something of a mystery. Their names might be bogus, too. I think they might have been in a Santa Fe hotel the night before the murder, though."

"Which one?"

"I don't know — possibly the Inn of the Anasazi. If not, then maybe one of the ones around the plaza. Could one of your people check that out?"

"I'll put a deputy on it right away. We can do that on the phone. What do you want me to do if I find them?"

"I doubt if you will find them, but you might get an address on them. If they paid by credit card, you could get that number and run it for a name and a billing address. You could try the rental car agencies, too."

"If, on the off chance, I actually can lay my hands on them, have you got anything to support a charge of murder?"

"I'm afraid not."

"Then how is it worth it to me to put a deputy on this? I can't arrest 'em for parting their hair funny."

"If you can tell me where to find them, I can put the NYPD onto them, and they might come up with something."

"Well, if they do come up with something worthwhile, I'm going to want these folks back in my county."

"There's an extradition process for that."

"Well, yeah."

"I'd appreciate your help, Ray. Maybe we can clear this one, get it off your books."

"I'd sure like that."

Stone gave him his number. "I'll look forward to hearing from you." The two men ended the conversation, and Stone hung up. He buzzed Joan.

"Yep?"

"Where is Carrie Fiske's stuff that was sent from New Mexico?"

"In the basement storage room."

"Can you ask Fred to bring all of it into my office?"

"Sure thing."

Ten minutes later Fred started carrying luggage into Stone's office; it took him three trips. "Anything else, sir?"

"Not at the moment," Stone said.

He put the largest suitcase on his desk and went methodically through it. Nothing but clothes, neatly packed. He went through the smaller case and found pretty much the same thing. The train case was all girl stuff. Her briefcase yielded an airplane e-ticket to New York, her passport, some keys, four checkbooks, some pens, and an envelope containing five thousand dollars in brand-new bills. He set it aside and went through the two photography cases, which contained, not surprisingly, cameras, lenses, film, and a tripod. In the larger case Stone found the 4×5 camera that he had seen on the floor in Carrie's rental cottage. He examined it carefully and found that it contained a plate. He stopped himself from pulling it out of the camera, not knowing how to determine if the plate had been exposed. He buzzed Joan.

"Yep?"

"Will you call Bob Cantor and ask him to drop by here when he gets a chance?"

"Does that mean right now?"

"If he's available."

She hung up and called him back three minutes later. "He's not far away — ten minutes."

"Good." Stone set the camera and case aside, picked up the handbag and emptied it onto his desktop. It contained everything he would expect to find in a woman's handbag: wallet, credit cards and cash, makeup, hairbrush, a guide to Ghost Ranch, and a checkbook. And an iPhone 6.

Joan buzzed. "Cantor's here, coming in."

Bob Cantor walked into the room. "You rang, Your Lordship?"

"What?"

"I heard you're a lord of the manor now."

"Put that out of your mind." He handed Cantor the camera. "This appears to have a plate in it, but I can't tell if it's been exposed, and I don't want to ruin it."

Cantor examined the camera, then he went to the case and found an aluminum plate, inserted it into the camera, and withdrew it with the plate attached. "There you go," he said.

"Has it been exposed?"

"I don't know. I can take it back to my darkroom and find out, and if it has, develop and print the shot."

"Thanks, I'd appreciate that."

Cantor left.

Stone picked up the iPhone and examined it. The number one appeared on the phone icon. He pressed it and found another number one on the voice mail icon. He pressed that and found a number. He pressed that, and a man's voice said, "Hey, Carrie, got your message. We'll see you around seven-thirty. Bye."

Stone noted the date and the phone number, then compared it to the one Nicky Chalmers had given him for the Bedfords. It was identical. He checked the recent calls and found a call to a 505 area code number; he pressed the I icon and the Hotel Santa Fe, Hacienda & Spa came up. He called Ray Martinez. "You don't have to do the search for the Bedford couple," he said. "They were at the Santa Fe Hotel and Hacienda, and they left a message confirming a dinner date with Ms. Fiske the night before I found her body. You still might try for an address."

"You done good," Martinez said.

47

Stone wasn't through with the iPhone; he pressed the photos icon and came up with dozens of photographs. He went carefully through them and was surprised to find his own face there: it had been taken at the East Hampton house. He looked through the same roll and found pictures of Nicky and Vanessa Chalmers and of Carrie Fiske, but there were no decent shots of Derek and Alicia Bedford. Each time a camera had been pointed at them they had managed to turn away or get a hand over their faces or otherwise prevent themselves from being photographed.

Joan buzzed. "Dino on one."

Stone pressed the button. "Tell me you've got news."

"I've got news, but not much. The Bedfords checked out of the Carlyle this morning. My people had a look at their suite and found the remains of a throwaway cell phone in a wastebasket, no SIM card."

"Can any data be recovered?"

"It's already in the lab, but they're not optimistic."

"I've got Carrie's cell phone, and there's a voice mail message that sounds like Derek, confirming a dinner date with her the night before I found her body. The call came from a Santa Fe hotel, and Sheriff Martinez is checking it out for an address, but given what you've just told me, I'm not hopeful."

"I have still more news," Dino said.

"Sorry I interrupted you."

"The names Derek and Alicia Bedford came up as aka's from the Palm Beach police, so we no longer know their names."

"How did they register at the Carlyle?"

"Hang on a minute."

"I'm hanging."

Dino came back. "They were registered as David and Alexandra Bannister and had a credit card that contained a number, but not a name. This sounds very much like the card is connected to a numbered account at an offshore bank that protects its clients with anonymity. The hotel looked at it askance, but it worked, so they didn't make a fuss."

"So we know their new names."

"For as long as they use them."

"I notice that the first initials of each name are the same as before. Why don't you canvass the high-end hotels for the new name, and if it isn't there, check for names beginning with D, A, and B?"

"You know something? You should have been a detective." Dino hung up.

Joan came on the phone. "Bob Cantor is on his way back here with a photograph," she said.

"Good news."

Bob arrived fifteen minutes later. "I've got something," he said, holding up an envelope. He fished out a photo. "It appears to have been taken with the camera on the floor, looking up. You can see beams across the ceiling." He held up a photograph of a man in left profile.

"Aha!" Stone said. "Progress. I found the camera on the floor of the cottage, and I speculated at the time that it may have been knocked over in a struggle."

"Looks like the camera went off when it hit the floor. Do you recognize the guy?"

"I do. It's somebody who called himself Derek Bedford, who has since changed his name to David Bannister."

"I've got more," Bob said. "I flopped the neg and printed it, so I've got a right profile." He held up the print. "Then through a little photographic legerdemain, I put the two profiles together and got a full face, sort of, but not exactly, since it's made up of two left profiles, and most people, if you draw a line down the middle of their faces and put two lefts or two rights together, look different."

"This one looks different," Stone said, "but it's a hell of a lot better than nothing, which is what we had five minutes ago." He buzzed Joan and asked her to fax the three photos to Dino, who called back in a flash.

"Where'd you get a photo of the guy?" he demanded.

Stone explained about the fallen camera and Bob's work on the negative.

"Okay, I'm going to get this distributed right now, and we can fax it to our list of hotels."

"You do that, pal, and maybe we'll get somewhere."

"Thanks for the photo. Now, have you got a motive for me?"

"I think they were after the Bloch-Bauer necklace, but it could just as well have been all of Carrie's jewelry. The guy must have tried to beat or choke the safe combination out of her. What he didn't know was that, in her purse, was a key to the apartment with a tab on the key ring that held the combination to the safe. He had it all and didn't know it."

"Where's her jewelry now?"

"At Sotheby's, where it will be auctioned. My appraiser says it's worth millions, something like a hundred pieces."

"Now we know what billionaires do with their money," Dino said.

"She's not even a billionaire. It just shows you that a girl can squeak by on a few hundred million bucks, until a billionaire comes along to take her away from all that."

"I could squeak by on a few hundred million," Dino said, "and you, my friend, are already doing just that."

"Then I confirm my own judgment."

"Okay, then tell me where to look for these two murderers."

"Well, we know they were in the city until this morning, but they could have left. Probably not to Palm Beach, since they seem to be already known to the police there. I'd say they're big-city people — L.A., Chicago, San Francisco, or maybe resort people — Aspen, Santa Barbara, like that. They seem to tend toward elegance and have expensive tastes. Maybe the FBI has something on them."

"I've already queried them, but I haven't had an answer yet. I'll bug them again. Talk to you later." Dino hung up.

"These people sound like they need the services of a good forger of identity documents," Bob said. "Would you like me to make some inquiries in the netherworld?"

"If you can do it without putting yourself at risk, Bob."

"I try to avoid that."

"Something just occurred to me," Stone said. "Don't you have some software that allows you to look at hotel registrations all over the place?"

"I do. They all seem to use one of about three software packages, and I've got an in with all three."

"Could you check current registrations for Derek and Alicia Bedford and for David and Alexandra Bannister?"

"As long as you don't tell the cops where you got the info."

"Of course not."

"I'll have to do this in my truck. Be back in a few."

Stone twiddled his thumbs for a few minutes, until Bob returned. "Mr. and Mrs. Bannister checked into the Lowell, on East Sixty-third, an hour ago." He gave Stone the suite number.

"Thank you, my friend," he said.

"Wait a little while before you call Dino,"

Bob said.

"If you think that will help."

"It might." Bob left.

Stone waited fifteen minutes, then called Dino.

48

Dino was on the phone in a flash. "Whataya got?"

"Don't ask me how I know this, but David and Alexandra Bannister are registered at the Lowell, on East Sixty-third."

"How do you know that?"

"You'll just have to trust me."

"That's on the same block as my apartment."

"I managed to figure that out." He gave Dino the suite number. "I'd like to go along for the bust. I can identify them."

"All right. Meet me there in an hour. It'll take me a while to get uptown, and I want the pleasure, myself."

"All right."

"We're going to do this softly, softly," Dino said. "No flashing lights or sirens, no uniforms, no gangs busting in all at once, got it?"

"I have not a light, a siren, or a uniform,

and I would make a poor gang member."

"When you see my car out front, get in and I'll tell you my plan."

"I can't wait to hear it."

Stone returned some calls, then started for the door.

"Don't forget," Joan said, stopping him in his tracks, "you have an appointment at four o'clock with Senator Marisa Bond."

"Damn it, I forgot about that."

"It's in your calendar, so that's no longer an excuse."

Stone got out of a cab at Sixty-third and Madison and spotted Dino's car parked across the street from the hotel. He rapped on the window, and Dino opened the door and invited him in.

"Okay, what's your plan?" Stone asked.

"You and I are going to go to the front desk and inquire as to whether Mr. and Mrs. Bannister are in, then I'm going to radio my team, and they'll filter in in twos."

"And what if they're not in?"

"Hang on, I'm still making this up. Okay, got it — we'll go up to their suite with a pass key and wait for them there."

"Have you got a warrant for this?"

"Have you forgotten that you're talking to

the police commissioner of the City of New York?"

"Nope. Have you got a warrant?"

"It'll be here in fifteen minutes."

"That's what I thought."

Half an hour later the warrant arrived in the hands of a breathless young patrolman in uniform.

"Get in the front seat," Dino said to the young man. "Didn't anybody tell you this is a plainclothes operation?"

"No, sir," the young cop said.

"Sheesh!" Dino picked up his radio. "Okay, Barrington and I are going in. Give us a five-minute head start." He got out of the car, and Stone followed. They walked into the hotel, and at the front desk Dino addressed the young woman on duty. "Good afternoon," he said. "Do you know who I am?"

She pointed at him. "Don't tell me . . . you're Joe Pesci, the actor!"

Stone burst out laughing.

Dino flashed his badge. "I'd like to see the manager, please."

She made the call. "He'll be right out." She pointed to Dino again. "Burgess Meredith!" she said.

"Mr. Meredith is a hundred years old, and a foot shorter than I am," Dino replied.

The manager appeared. "May I help you? Oh, Commissioner, good day to you."

"Good day." Dino exposed a corner of an envelope in his inside jacket pocket. "This is a warrant," he said. "Are Mr. and Mrs. David Bannister in their suite?"

"No, sir," the desk clerk said, "they went out for some lunch."

"Then I'd like a key to their suite, please."

"Do it," the manager said to the young woman, and she printed out a key card.

Dino put it in his jacket pocket. "Half a dozen other men will be joining me in just a minute," he said.

"The elevators are there," she replied, pointing.

Stone and Dino rang for an elevator; it arrived shortly, and they got in. As the doors began to close, a hand stopped them, and a couple got in. The doors closed, and the elevator started up.

Stone suddenly realized who they were. "Derek, Alicia," he said, extending his hand. "It's Stone Barrington."

They didn't miss a beat, and for a moment it was old home week. "Are you staying here, Stone?"

"Visiting friends," Stone said. The elevator doors opened and Stone followed them out. "Oh, I'm sorry," he said, "let me introduce my friend Dino Bacchetti." Hands were shaken and smiles exchanged. "Dino," Stone said, "is the police commissioner of New York City, and he has a warrant for your arrest."

Derek/David put his key card in the door to his suite and opened it. "Come in, and let's chat. After you, Commissioner."

Dino entered, followed by Stone, and the door slammed behind them.

"Shit!" Dino yelled, yanking on the door. It wouldn't open.

"He's jammed it," Stone said, trying to help. They were still working on it when there was a sharp rap on the door. "Police! Open up!"

"Put your shoulder against it!" Dino yelled. A couple of tries, and the door burst open.

"A handkerchief," Stone said, pointing to it on the floor. "I didn't know you could jam a door with a handkerchief."

"Everybody downstairs!" Dino commanded. "You guys take the stairs." He pressed the elevator button as the four cops headed down the stairs.

Dino got on the radio. "The subjects are on their way downstairs!" he yelled into it. They got onto the elevator, rode down, and emerged into the lobby. All was perfectly peaceful. A moment later four plainclothes cops burst out of the door to the stairs, pistols drawn.

"Find 'em!" Dino yelled.

Stone and Dino hurried to the street and looked both ways. Nothing.

Stone looked at his watch. "Listen," he said, "I've got an appointment with a United States senator in half an hour. Let me know how this turns out." He ran for a cab, leaving Dino fuming on the sidewalk, shouting into his radio.

49

Stone passed a limo parked outside his house and hurried into his office. "She's waiting," Joan said. He took a deep breath, calmed himself, and went in.

Senator Marisa Bond sat in a leather chair in his seating area, her surprisingly long legs stretched out before her. Bob sat beside her, his head in her lap. "Good afternoon, Mr. Barrington," she said, offering her hand.

Stone took it: firm grip, long fingers. "I see you and Bob have become acquainted." He studiously avoided looking down her cleavage and suppressed all carnal thoughts, which wasn't easy, since she was more beautiful than she looked on TV.

"We've had a very nice conversation," she replied.

"May I offer you some coffee?" he asked, glancing at his watch. "Or something more medicinal?"

"It's been a long day," she replied. "Do

you have a bourbon-flavored medicinal?"

"I do," Stone said, grateful for the opportunity to have a drink himself. He poured them both one, picked up her file from his desk, and sat down on the sofa, opposite her. They raised their glasses and drank.

"I should have been the senator from Kentucky, instead of Virginia," she said.

Stone laughed. "Have you been in town long?"

"Only since this morning. I took the shuttle up to do some fund-raising. I don't get to come to New York often enough to suit me. Next time there's a vacant Senate seat here, I'll give some thought to changing states. You aren't recording any of this, are you?"

"Not a word. The President asked me to meet with you."

"And me to meet with you."

Stone glanced at her curriculum vitae: "Smith College, valedictorian. Harvard Law, editor of the *Law Review,* then a doctorate in constitutional law. And I see that in your years of private practice you pled cases before the Supreme Court more than a hundred times before being appointed solicitor general by Will Lee, and in that position you appeared before the Court

286

another sixty-odd times."

"I sound so well qualified when you say it like that," she replied with a chuckle.

"Tell me, are your views on all the hot-button issues well known, or have you been terribly discreet about that?"

"I'm a Democrat," she replied. "I think that about covers it."

"So, if I asked you how you would vote on a particular case, how would you reply?"

"I would decline to reply, since the subject might come up if I were on the Court. I think the President is well aware of how I think."

"As are the members of the Senate Judiciary Committee?"

"Oh, yes. I serve on that committee."

"How do you get along with the Republican members?"

"I flatter them at every opportunity," she said. "I'd show a little leg, if it would help."

Stone laughed. This wasn't going the way he had imagined it would. "Is there anything in your views that might surprise the President, not to mention the committee?"

Senator Bond thought about that. "You may have noticed that when I mentioned guns, I referred to 'gun safety'?"

"I did notice that."

"It wouldn't bother me if every qualified

American went around armed, if I could choose who was qualified. What I mean to say is, I'd let eighty or ninety percent of the population carry a concealed weapon after serious training, but I'd make it a lot harder to get a carry license, and I'd make them renewable annually, just to see who was serious. Of course, that's more a legislative view than one from the court, but still, it might surprise the President."

"Well," Stone said, "it's probably better that she hear that from me, instead of when a split decision was announced."

"I'll grant you that."

"Is there anything in your personal life that she should know about?"

"I had a nasty divorce twelve years ago. My former husband is dead, and I didn't shoot him, but still, he told some hurtful lies about me at the time, and I'm sure that's in somebody's opposition research handbook."

"Have you remarried?"

"No, and if I should decide to do so, I'd have a broad field to choose from, because it could go either way, regarding gender."

That stopped Stone in his tracks. "And what percentage of the population knows that about you?"

"Exactly two women and one man, including you."

"And are the two women discreet?"

"One is dead, and you can't get any more discreet than that. The other is married to a United States senator, has been for twenty-odd years, and I don't think she'd want her children to know."

"Would you want the President to know about that, going in?"

"I'm afraid I'm not going to make it easy for you, Mr. Barrington. If I had my druthers, I'd wait until I was confirmed before I let it out, but now I've done my duty by reporting it to the President's man, and both you and she can do with it what you will, and I'll not give a damn. May I have another drink?"

Stone was happy to get up and get her another, since it would give him a moment to recover. He poured them both another one and sat down again. "Anything else I should know about?"

"No bestiality or child porn in my past, present, or future. I've never committed a crime that didn't involve a radar gun on a highway, and I don't use drugs of any sort, except alcohol, and I never have more than two drinks in a twenty-four-hour period, so I won't ask for another." She raised her glass and drank.

They spent the remainder of their hour together chatting about whatever came up, and Stone liked her more and more. Finally, he and Bob walked her to her car, and he put her inside. He waved her off, regretting that circumstances didn't allow him to be more forward.

50

Stone had dinner with Dino at Rotisserie Georgette, an East Side favorite of his that specialized in French comfort food. Viv was out of town on business.

"The *Times* reviewer said that the clock in this place stopped at ten minutes before *cuisine nouvelle,*" Stone remembered.

"That's good enough for me," Dino said, and they split a roast chicken between them.

"Okay, what happened after I left you at the Lowell?"

"Turns out that David and Alexandra, as they then were, ducked into the restaurant next door through the hotel lobby entrance, and the doorman there put them into a cab. We missed them by a whisker, and those New York yellow cabs have a way of all looking alike."

"Did you shoot any of your entourage?"

"Nah, it wasn't their fault, it was yours, for not figuring that trick with the door."

"I assume you exercised your rights under the search warrant?"

"I did. We took the suite apart, but there was nothing there but clothes and the sort of things people travel with."

"No fake IDs or paperwork of any kind?"

"You tell me — was the guy carrying a briefcase when they got on the elevator with us?"

"Jesus, I think you're right. I forgot about that."

"Then that's where the goodies were. I'd give a lot to rummage through that brief-case."

"Would you like me to do my magic trick and find out if they've checked into another hotel?"

"You mean get Bob Cantor to use his ill-gotten computer program?"

"I did *not* say that."

"Did you know that in France, when anyone checks into a hotel, a little card is filled out, and those are collected every evening by the local cop shop, and all the names entered into their computer?"

"I did know that, but I'd forgotten it. You should buy Bob's computer program, you know."

"We would, if he hadn't stolen parts of it from half a dozen other pieces of copyrighted software. He'd have to rewrite all the code from scratch before we'd touch it, and that could take months, if not years."

"It might be worth the wait," Stone pointed out.

"But to get back to the subject at hand. I don't think D and A are in a hotel, I think they've got a little hidey-hole somewhere in the city, probably not far from the Lowell and the Carlyle, where they keep their wardrobe and the tools of their trade — computer, cameras, color copying machine, laminator, et cetera, plus checkbooks, letters of credit, and all the other paraphernalia that the modern con artiste employs."

"I would have thought they'd be out of town by now."

"Nah, we did some digging and found traces of them here and there. They're supremely confident, those two. Did you notice how cool D was when you introduced me? And believe me, they had already planned an escape route out of that hotel or they wouldn't have been staying there. It was like they went up in a puff of smoke."

"So what's your next move?"

"I don't have one," Dino admitted, "but I wouldn't be surprised if we heard from them again. By 'we' I mean 'you.' "

"Why would they contact me?"

"To gloat, maybe."

"You think they're that cocky?"

"Oh, hell yes. I expect they've made a very nice living, maybe a fortune, out of what they do, and they admire themselves."

"That reminds me — I had a call from my New Mexico sheriff. He checked with the hotel, and they used a credit card there with no customer or bank name on it, just a number and the usual strip of magnetic tape."

"And what does that tell you?"

"They've got an offshore bank account — maybe in the Cayman Islands, maybe more than one place. They can wire-transfer funds into it from anywhere, and they can use the anonymous card to get cash at ATMs, or use it at hotels, rental car agencies, and like that."

"That sounds pretty smooth," Dino said. "I'd like to have one of those."

"All you need is a ticket to the Bahamas, where you charter a light airplane to fly you to George Town, Caymans — and enough cash in your bag to impress a banker. You need never visit the bank again."

"How long do you suppose they've been doing this work?"

"They're in their late forties, early fifties, I'd say, and I'll bet that at least one of them has worked in a bank or on Wall Street. They'd need that kind of experience to work their scams."

"Did they take Carrie Fiske for any money?"

"I think they had planned to, but once they got a whiff of her jewelry collection, they probably ditched the long con they usually run and went for the ice. But they got greedy and impatient and killed the golden goose."

"And what do you think they're doing now?"

"Looking for another goose."

51

Stone got up a little early the following morning to greet his next person of interest for the Big Court. This was Congressman Terrence Maher, the bane of the House Ways and Means Committee.

Stone found him drinking coffee and reading a *Washington Post* (his own) on the sofa in his office. Bob watched him carefully from a respectful distance.

"Good morning. I'm Stone Barrington."

"Terry Maher," the man said. He was short, thick, and pugnacious-looking, with short, thick, graying hair and a poorly reconstructed broken nose.

"Can I get you more coffee?"

"You don't want to experience me on *two* cups of coffee," Maher replied.

Stone picked up the Maher folder on his desk and sat down. "Let's see — City College of New York, BBA in accounting, Columbia Law and law review. Eight years with the late, great accounting firm of Arthur Andersen & Co., then ran for Congress in the Tenth District, formerly the home of Ed Koch and Carmine DeSapio. If I hadn't grown up and moved uptown, you'd be my congressman."

"And you would be a lucky citizen," Maher said.

"You look like a former pug."

"U.S. Marine Corps middleweight champion. I've put on a little tonnage since those days."

"What was it like being gay in the Marine Corps?"

"It would have been hell on earth and probably fatal, if they had found out, but I managed to keep it quiet until I ran for Congress, then the *Post* unearthed an old lover — not even a very good one — and almost blew me out of the water. I think the gay vote in the Village saved me, and I've been eternally grateful to them ever since. I even tried to get the Stonewall Inn made a national monument — nearly drove the Republicans crazy."

"You living with anybody now?"

"Hell, I'm married to a really sweet guy, another ex-Marine, nearly a year, now."

"Congratulations. Does that leave anything in your personal life that might embarrass the President during the confirmation hearings?"

"Oh, the *Post* dragged all that out years ago. I've got some scar tissue, but no sucking wounds."

"How do you see the hearings going? Any hope of getting confirmed?"

"As long as I don't make an ass of myself while testifying, I don't think they'd dare give me much trouble. The tide has turned and come roaring in, and they know that a vote against me would cause demonstrations in their districts. On the other hand, a vote for me would give them a leg to stand on come election day."

"What about questions on more substantive issues?"

"All they can say is that I don't follow their ideology, and I've voted on the moderate-to-conservative side of enough issues to give me some shade to stand in. Also, I've helped out every member of that committee in one way or another over the years. They're not going to treat me as an embarrassment. I might even make it easy for them — get a suit made and grow a better haircut for the hearings."

"Couldn't hurt," Stone said. "Remember, they'll be showing all that on TV for years to come — might as well look good."

"Let me ask you something," Maher said.

"Shoot."

"How'd I end up getting vetted in *your* office. I didn't even know who the hell you were until I asked around."

"What did you hear back?"

"Lawyer at a top firm, used to be married to the widow of a movie star — that's about it."

"To answer your question, the President asked me to meet you and report back."

"Yeah, but why *you*?"

"I understand you're meeting four people, and I don't know who the others are, but I would guess they're people she knows well and from whom she can expect a straight answer to her questions."

"Fair enough. Are you seeing Tiffany Baldwin?"

"Yes."

"Would you believe that she once tried to put the make on *me*? How crazy is she?"

"An excellent question. Maybe she doesn't read the *Post.*"

"I guess not. I wouldn't want to go three rounds with her, either. I'm not sure I'd walk away."

"Your instincts are good, Terry."

"What else do you want to know? I've got a record — the President knows what I'm for and against."

"What's likely to come up in the hearings that might surprise her?"

Maher thought about that. "I'm one hell of a good cook," he said. "French, Italian, anything you like."

"Well, that surprises *me.*"

"I've often thought that when somebody finally unseats me — not that that's possible — I might open a restaurant."

"I'll be your first customer." Stone stood up and offered his hand. "Good to meet you."

"And you." Maher left; Bob watched him go but didn't move.

"And what's the matter with you, Bob? That guy scare you?"

The tail did the talking.

Joan buzzed. "Tiffany Baldwin in half an hour. I tried to get her to do it in public, but she wouldn't budge."

"All right. When she gets here I want you to come in here with a steno pad."

"You know I don't do shorthand."

"Pretend, and don't leave her alone with me for a second."

52

Stone was waiting for Tiffany Baldwin to arrive when Joan buzzed him. "Somebody named Daryl Barnes is on line one. He says you know him."

"I don't."

"Want me to get rid of him?"

Stone had a thought. "No, and call in that number Dino gave us and ask for a trace." He waited for a slow count of ten, then pressed the button. "Mr. Barnes? This is Stone Barrington."

"Hello, Stone."

"Have we met?"

"Several times, most recently at the Lowell."

"Ah, are we using real names now?"

"It's what my mama put on my birth certificate," he said, and with a Southern accent.

"And is that a real accent?"

"It's the way I used to talk, before I was

led astray by Yankees."

"How about . . . what's your wife's name?"

"Annie Allen, though we haven't had the benefit of clergy. Yes, she's a Southerner. We're both from a little town called Delano, Georgia."

"I've heard of it," Stone said. "Meriwether County, isn't it?"

"I'm impressed. I wouldn't have thought your geography lessons in school would have covered Meriwether County."

"It's a pretty name, it stuck in my mind, I guess." Stone looked at his watch; at least a minute gone.

"I suppose you're wondering why I called."

"Actually, Commissioner Bacchetti predicted you would."

"Did he? The man's clairvoyant!"

"Just very smart."

"Why did he think I would call?"

"Because you're cocky."

That got a laugh. "Well, he's nailed me, I guess."

"If he hasn't, he will. It's what he does."

"I must say, I was flattered that the commissioner of police came personally to arrest me."

"He lives down the block from the Lowell — I guess he wanted his neighborhood's air freshened."

"Now, let's not get nasty. I called because I want to hire you."

"For what purpose?"

"To defend me against the charge the commissioner came to arrest me for, whatever it is."

"I'm afraid I have a conflict of interest," Stone said.

"What conflict?"

"I represent the estate of the victim."

"What estate? What victim?"

"Come now, Mr. Barnes, disingenuousness doesn't suit you."

"I'm afraid you've baffled me."

"The murder of Carrie Fiske."

"Wait a minute — Carrie is dead?"

Stone checked his watch again: two minutes.

"Tell you what, I'll hear your alibi and give you some advice, no charge."

"When and where was she killed? I'll give you my alibi."

"Later in the evening, after your dinner date with her."

"Last time I had dinner with Carrie, you were there, in East Hampton."

"Then how is it that the police have a voice message on her phone from you, confirming dinner?"

"Dinner where?"

"In New Mexico. Nicky Chalmers puts you there, too."

"We left New Mexico an hour after I saw Nicky."

"Oh, and here's the kicker — the police have a photograph of you at the scene of her death, and it's date-stamped."

There was silence at the other end.

"Remember the camera and tripod you knocked over? It went off, and got a very nice likeness."

"I think I'd better be going," he said.

"But you haven't had my free advice."

"Okay, what is it?"

"Give yourself up, tell the police everything, and I'll recommend a good lawyer to represent you. With a little luck, he might get the charge reduced to manslaughter."

"Thanks, I don't think so."

"You could be out in ten years, or so."

"Oh, swell."

"It beats life in the New Mexico State Prison, which is not the sort of elegant hostelry you're accustomed to."

Another silence, then . . . "Who's the lawyer?"

"Ed Eagle, of Santa Fe. He's in the phone book. There is none better west of the Mississippi — maybe not east of, either."

304

"I've heard of him."

"What other charges against you are current? Is there a line of prosecutors waiting?"

"I have never been charged with any crime," he said.

"Then how did you come to the attention of the Palm Beach police?"

"That was a misunderstanding, quickly cleared up."

"What sort of misunderstanding?"

"It doesn't matter."

"Perhaps it doesn't. But Carrie Fiske matters, I can promise you that."

"Goodbye, Mr. Barrington." He hung up.

Stone buzzed Joan. "Tell Dino, if that wasn't long enough for him to trace, he's fired."

53

Joan buzzed. "Ms. Tiffany Baldwin to see you."

"Show her in, and remember what I said."

A blond head was stuck around his doorjamb. "Knock, knock?"

"Come in, Tiffany," he said, extending a hand to be shaken.

She brushed it aside and came into his arms. "Hello, cutie," she said, rubbing herself against his crotch.

Behind her, Joan produced a coughing fit. Tiffany turned and glared at her.

"Take the sofa, Tiffany, Joan can take the chair." He picked up her folder and pretended to study it while she decided what to do. Finally, she sat down. Joan was ready with her steno pad.

"I don't want to keep you from the business of the nation for too long, so let's get started." He glanced at the folder. "Columbia undergraduate and Columbia Law

School, assistant district attorney under the esteemed Robert Morgenthau for eight years, then chief prosecutor — a fairly meteoric rise, I'd say."

"Thank you, Mr. Barrington," she said archly.

"Then assistant U.S. attorney for another six, and lo and behold, you're appointed to the big job — United States attorney for the Southern District of New York."

"That is correct, as you well know."

"What would you say is the hallmark of your time in that office?"

"Fighting crime — decimating organized crime in my jurisdiction."

"Did you deal much with constitutional issues, as opposed to criminal prosecutions?"

"Whenever those issues arose."

"Lifelong Democrat?"

"No, I was a Republican until I went to work for Mr. Morgenthau. He showed me the error of my ways."

"Good for Mr. Morgenthau. Tell me, what would the President be surprised to hear about you?"

Her eyebrows went up. "You could tell her as well as I."

Joan coughed again and pretended to write down something.

"Anything more apropos to the occasion?"

"She might be surprised by my liberal bent on the bench."

"But you've never served on any bench. Would you say you've been a liberal prosecutor?"

"The law doesn't allow for political preferences, it's just enforced."

"Good point. Is there anything you would not like to come up during the vetting process?"

"My personal life," she said. "Or yours."

That sounded like a threat to Stone. "My life doesn't enter into it."

"I'm sure you would prefer that it didn't."

"Is there anything more the President should know about your background?"

"My life is an open book."

I certainly hope not, Stone thought. "I'll tell her you said so. Is there anything else you'd like to include in our conversation?"

"Not in the present company," she replied, her eyes drilling through Joan. "Perhaps if we could meet alone."

"I don't think that will be necessary," Stone said. "That completes the interview." He stood up, and so did Joan. "Joan, will you show Ms. Baldwin out, please?" He offered his hand again, this time with the coffee table between them. "Good to see you,

Tiffany."

Joan managed to keep herself between Stone and his guest as she showed the woman to the door. Stone heard her lock it behind Tiffany, then she returned.

"That woman is a piece of work," she said. "I thought she was going to jump you right here in front of me."

"Thank you, Joan, that will be all. Oh, get me Dino, will you, please?" He settled behind his desk and waited for the phone to buzz, which it did. "Good morning. I hope we gave your people enough time to trace that call."

"Oh, yes, plenty of time," Dino said. "He was driving down Park Avenue, presumably in a cab. He got off at Forty-fourth Street."

"No luck, then?"

"None."

"Well, I got luckier, I think."

"You think? Don't you know when you get lucky?"

"He told me his real name — his girl-friend's, too. He says they're not married."

"I've got a pencil."

"He says his name is Daryl Barnes, and hers is Annie Allen. To hear him tell it they were childhood sweethearts in a small town in Georgia called Delano, in Meriwether County."

"What makes you think he told you his real name?"

"He wanted me to represent him. By the way, he denied all knowledge of Carrie's murder, until I told him we had his voice on her iPhone and the photograph of him at the scene. Then he came over all quiet."

"I would have been happier if a DA had surprised him with that information."

"I was trying to get his real name."

"Hang on a minute." Dino made typing noises. "Nothing on him," he said.

"He told me he'd never been arrested before, that whatever happened in Palm Beach was a misunderstanding, quickly resolved."

"Wait a minute, we've got a bite on an Ann Allen. She was picked up in an Atlanta hotel fifteen years ago for running the badger game on an undercover cop. Her partner got away clean, and since she didn't have a record, she got a thousand-dollar fine and a year, suspended. Her fine was paid by a Daryl Jones, in cash. We've got nothing on a Daryl Jones."

"So maybe his name is Daryl Barnes — maybe he changed it for the occasion."

"Sounds that way to me."

"You want me to run Daryl Barnes

through a computer program I know about?"

"You mean the computer program I've never heard of?"

"That's the one."

"I can't stop you."

"I'll get back to you." Stone called Bob Cantor and waited while he ran the name against hotel registrants.

"Nothing," Cantor said.

"See you." Stone hung up and called Dino. "No Daryl Barnes registered at any New York hotel."

"Well, shit. If you're going to use an illegal means of search, you might at least try to use one that works."

"Dino, that makes as much sense as anything you've ever said to me." Stone hung up.

54

Joan came into Stone's office bearing an envelope. "This just arrived by messenger from Sotheby's."

Stone opened the envelope and found another. Inside that was an invitation printed on heavy cream paper:

The Board of Directors of Sotheby's
requests the pleasure of your company
at a private showing of jewelry from
the estate of Carrie Fiske,
to include the first sight
in three-quarters of a century of the
diamond-and-ruby necklace worn
by Adele Bloch-Bauer
in the *Gold* painting by Gustav Klimt

The date and time were for three days hence. Stone had a sudden thought. He called Jamie Niven at Sotheby's.

"Good afternoon, Stone. I trust you

received your invitation to the private show-ing."

"I did, thank you, and I am responding. I will attend with pleasure."

"This is going to be a real do. Have you seen any of the publicity?"

"Everywhere and constantly. Jamie, you're doing a great job."

"Thank you. Anything else I can do for you?"

"Jamie, I assume that you have a comput-erized list of the people Sotheby's does busi-ness with."

"We have."

"Would you search a name for me, please?"

"Of course.

"Daryl Barnes." Stone spelled it for him.

Clicking of keys. "Yes, we do. He's never bought anything, but he requested to be notified of important jewelry sales."

"Do you have an address for Mr. Barnes?"

"We do. He resides at 740 Park Avenue."

That stopped Stone in his tracks; that was the address of Carrie Fiske's apartment. "Are you positive of that?"

"I am."

"Would you be kind enough to dispatch an invitation to the private showing to Mr. Barnes?"

"If you wish it, of course."

"Tell me, Jamie, what sort of security will you have for such an event?"

"We have four levels of security. This will be Level One, the highest, because of the allure of the Bloch-Bauer necklace," he said. "It would only go higher if the President or the Pope were attending."

"How many of them will be in some sort of uniform?"

"Only two, who will be stationed near the necklace. Everyone else will be in plain-clothes."

"May I make a suggestion?"

"Of course."

"Put those two in plainclothes, too, and don't use your largest men."

"What did you have in mind, Stone?"

"An attempt to steal the necklace."

"Do you know something I don't?"

"Mr. Daryl Barnes may be the murderer of Carrie Fiske, and he is a lover of fine jewelry."

Jamie made an odd sound. "Well, in that case, I think we'd better have a police presence, don't you?"

"I do, but I don't think it should be obvious. May I make those arrangements for you? The commissioner and I are old friends."

"Thank you, yes."

"And if you don't mind, I won't make the nature of that presence known to anyone else at Sotheby's but you."

"That's a very odd suggestion. Why not?"

"Well, if I were a jewel thief, I would do my very best to suborn a well-placed person on your staff. Wouldn't you?"

"While I resent the implication, I believe I would."

"This means you must not tell a soul that the police will be there. This is black tie, right?"

"Right, and I will keep the police presence to myself."

"I'll arrange a meeting between Dino and his people and you, but not at Sotheby's. They will want to see the layout of the viewing at that time."

"All right, I'll produce that on request."

"And please hand-deliver Mr. Barnes's invitation."

"It will be there inside an hour."

"Thank you, Jamie." He hung up and called Dino.

"Bacchetti."

"I think we may have had something of a break."

"Tell me about it."

Stone did.

"You're guessing."

"Guessing is all that is left to us, is it not?"

"I guess you're right."

"Then you'd better get some of your people over to the tuxedo rental place, and it would be a good idea to have as many female officers as males. We want elegant-looking couples, not a lot of apes in black tie standing around waiting for something terrible to happen. It might make Mr. Barnes nervous."

55

Stone looked up a White House number and found the direct line for Paul Kale, a young man who was one of three secretaries to the President. He dialed the number.

"Paul Kale."

"Good morning, Paul, this is Stone Barrington. How are you?"

"Very well, thank you, Mr. Barrington, and you?"

"Very well. Can you tell me if the President is available at this hour? She asked me to call."

"If you will kindly hold, I'll see if she can talk. I know she's expecting your call."

"Of course." Stone waited for about a minute and a half, then Katharine Lee came on the line.

"Stone!"

"Good morning, Madam President."

"Please, it's Kate when we're alone."

"I know, but I have trouble with that."

"Get over it or I'll hang up on you."

"I'm over it, Kate."

"Have you a report for me?"

"I do. You asked not to have it in writing."

"I did. Speak to me."

"Very well. First, Tiffany Baldwin. Ms. Baldwin is an outstanding prosecuting attorney with no judicial experience. She seems to be best in black-and-white situations, which lends itself to criminal prosecution, but perhaps not the bench. She lacks subtlety in every part of her life that I am familiar with, and I have known her for some years. In a confirmation hearing, the question of judicial temperament will surely be raised, and justly so. In those circumstances she is likely to respond to questions in a manner demonstrating her complete lack of such temperament. Need I continue?"

"I don't think so. I've heard similar but less blunt assertions from others about her. Continue?"

"Next is Senator Marisa Bond, with whom I was very impressed."

Kate laughed. "I rather thought you would be."

"Impressed in every possible way. She is highly intelligent, has spectacular credentials, and a temperament that would go a long way toward giving the Court a more collegial atmosphere. In spite of her liberal leanings, she has made a continuous effort over the years to get along with Republicans without necessarily going along. For this reason, I think confirmation would be quick."

"I'm delighted to hear you say that. Anything else?"

"Yes. Senator Bond went out of her way to convey to me that her sexual preferences are, well, broad."

"Oh? That surprises me."

"I believe she told me this in response to a question of what might surprise you about her. She also made it clear that she has exercised her tastes in a highly limited and very discreet manner. There is only one living female partner in her past, who is the wife of a sitting senator — she didn't say which one. I had the impression that, once confirmed, she might be less discreet in that regard, but we must remember that she likes men, too."

"She had a bad marriage, I believe."

"She did. It ended twelve years ago with recriminations on the part of her former husband that she says were outright lies. He died two years after their divorce. It's possible that opposition research might unearth some of the man's comments."

"It was a long time ago, and she's conducted her life impeccably since that time."

"I agree."

"So you think she's a serious candidate?"

"I think she's a very fine one, though it occurs to me that women are already well represented on the court."

"That has to be considered. What did you think of Terry Maher?"

"I liked him enormously, as I have often in his television appearances. He is frank to the point of bluntness, charming when he wants to be, and very, very smart. He offsets being gay with a macho mien, which was well-earned in the U.S. Marines, in his youth. I don't know whether you're aware that he was the middleweight boxing champion of his service."

"I am aware of that. I like it, too, that he retired as a gunnery sergeant, not a colonel."

"He didn't mention that to me, but it's a good point."

"So, Stone, do you have a preference among the three?"

"Maher."

"No doubts?"

"None. He's made a very successful effort, like Senator Bond, of getting along with his opposition, and I think that after the uproar from the right wing about his gayness has subsided, he would be easily confirmed and look good doing it on television. He's also only in his mid-forties, so given good health, he'd be on the Court for a very long time."

"I invited him to a State dinner a few weeks ago, and I loved it that he and his husband turned up in their Marine dress uniforms. Lots of ribbons."

"That must have been a sight. Is there anything else I can do for you, Kate?"

"Yes. Will and I are going to be in New York this week and we thought we might attend the showing of Ms. Fiske's jewelry at Sotheby's. Will you come with us?"

"I would be delighted."

"Have you a date?"

"No."

"I'm sure Holly Barker would love to attend. Shall I bring her with us?"

"That would be wonderful!"

"Oh, good! She works far too hard on the National Security Council. Once in a while I have to take her away, just to be sure she has some fun in her life." Kate paused. "I believe she has a New York apartment."

"She does, but it's small and cramped."

"I trust I won't have to put her in a hotel."

"Certainly not. I'll see that she's made . . .

comfortable."

"Thank you so much, Stone. Come for a drink at the Carlyle and we'll have dinner afterward. Say, five o'clock?"

"I'd be delighted."

"Goodbye, then, and give Holly a call."

"I will certainly do so. Goodbye, Kate." He hung up and called Holly's direct extension at the White House.

"Holly Barker."

"It's Stone. I've been reliably informed that you will be in New York this week, and that, if I play my cards right, I might have the pleasure of your company."

"That depends. How are you planning to play your cards?"

"Is this phone call being recorded?"

"Thank you, no further details will be required. I'll see you in Turtle Bay late tomorrow afternoon."

"I will look forward to that."

"May we see Dino and Viv?"

"That will be my next call."

They said goodbye and hung up.

56

The following day Holly arrived a little late, so they had only half an hour in bed before they had to dress for dinner.

"I apologize for the brevity," Holly said.

"You have nothing to apologize for," Stone said, kissing her, then watching as she got out of bed and padded around the master suite, collecting garments for the evening, followed everywhere by Bob. He and Holly were already in love. She gave him a little wave, then headed for the shower.

They arrived at Patroon nearly on time. Dino and Viv were only half a drink ahead of them. Everybody kissed, while Bob explained to a waiter about his bone.

"It's very good to see you back home," Dino said to Holly.

"Oh, Washington is my home now," she replied.

"You still have an apartment here, don't you?"

"Yes, but I never use it," she said, winking at Stone. "Besides, I'm told it's a good investment, already worth twice what I paid for it."

"Speaking of apartments," Dino said, "our friend Daryl Barnes doesn't have one at 740 Park."

"I'm not surprised," Stone said. "Maybe he has friends there?"

"Marks, maybe — friends, no. And we can't go canvassing the building, asking the residents if they have any guests who are con men and murderers. The mayor would be on the horn in seconds."

"Have you had your meeting with the Sotheby's security people?"

"Yeah, this afternoon. I think we've got it bracketed."

"How many of your officers will be there?"

"Four. Sotheby's will have another four."

"And there'll be a dozen Secret Service people in the building," Holly added.

"Oh, are the Lees coming?"

"They are. Kate says Christmas is only a few months away, and Will needs to be exposed to jewelry well ahead of time."

"That's a pretty broad hint," Viv said.

"Kate doesn't believe in little hints where

jewelry is concerned."

"Smart girl," Viv said, digging an elbow into Dino's ribs.

"Oh, I forgot," Dino said. "We'll be there, too — strictly out of security concerns."

"It can't hurt to have a look at Carrie's jewels," Viv pointed out.

"Oh, yes it can," Dino replied.

"Another nice thing about having the Secret Service there," Holly said, "is that every person in the room and every staff member will have been okayed by them before the President arrives. They will have run the name, date of birth, and Social Security number on everyone, and anybody with a criminal record or who has ever threatened a president will be excluded."

"That should help make security easier," Dino said.

"I'm looking forward to seeing the Bloch-Bauer necklace," Viv said.

"You could have stopped by my office and seen it there," Stone said, "until I turned it over to Sotheby's."

"I don't recall an invitation," she said, glaring at Dino.

"It never occurred to me that you would want to see it," he said.

"*See it?* Everybody in New York wants to see it. I want to wear it out to dinner."

"Not without an armed guard," Stone said.

"You forget, I'm in the armed guard business. I could have a platoon of them guarding me."

"Dino," Stone said, "you are clearly remiss."

"Thank you for your support," Dino replied.

"Viv," Stone said, "maybe after the reception I can arrange for you to try on the necklace."

Holly's hand shot up. "Me too!"

"All right, you too."

"They can arm-wrestle for it," Dino said. "I'd like to watch that."

"You can go first, Viv," Holly said.

"You, my dear, are a gentlewoman of the first water," Viv said, clinking glasses with her.

"Stone," Dino said, "you should bid on the necklace."

"Me? What would I do with a ten-million-dollar piece of jewelry?"

"Want a suggestion?" Holly asked, snuggling up to him.

"Tell you what," Stone said, "I'll bid on it, and you and Viv can take turns wearing it . . ."

This received a chorus of cheers.

". . . if Dino will pay the insurance premiums."

"Yeah, sure," Dino said.

"I want you both to remember that I made the offer," Stone said, "and that Dino wouldn't hold up his end."

"Tell you what," Dino said, "I won't pay the insurance, but I'll be sure that whoever is wearing it will have an armed guard from the NYPD."

More cheers from the women.

"Until I retire."

Groans from the women.

Dinner arrived and was consumed.

57

Stone and Holly were getting dressed for the jewelry showing in their separate dressing rooms.

"Viv phoned me," Holly called across the master bedroom. "The Lees invited them to dinner, too. They're going to pick us up at four forty-five."

"Great," Stone called back. "Nice to have a police escort."

"I don't get nearly enough of those," Holly called back.

"Not even traveling with Kate?"

"Mine is a White House job. I don't travel with her that much, unless we're in the middle of some foreign crisis."

Stone adjusted his bow tie and stepped into the bedroom. Holly was having a last look at her spectacular red dress. "Wow! Where do you find these clothes?"

"I never have time for a day of shopping, so if I see something I like in a shop window,

I buy it and save it for when I get one of these invitations, so I've always got something to wear."

"Smart girl. Where do you get the money to buy three-thousand-dollar dresses, if you don't mind my asking."

"Not at all. I make a decent salary, and I have my army pension on top of that." She looked at him coyly. "And I have money you don't know about."

"Oh? And where did that come from?"

"I found it in a tree."

"Not at the end of a rainbow?"

"No, in a tree — literally."

"Kindly explain."

"I'll tell you one of these days, when I've had a few drinks."

"I love a mysterious woman." He looked at his watch again. "We'd better get downstairs."

As they reached the front door, Dino's big black SUV glided to a halt out front, followed by an unmarked police car. They got into the rear seat.

"Very nice, Dino!" Holly enthused.

"It's only my due," Dino replied. "I'm a terribly important person."

"Don't ever retire," Viv said. "I like the car."

They arrived at the Carlyle and, accompanied by a Secret Service agent, took an elevator to the Lees' apartment. A butler opened the door and they found former President Will Lee, in a tuxedo, with an infant in his arms.

"May I introduce William Henry Lee the Fifth, called Will Henry, after his great-grandfather?"

Viv and Holly made oohing and aahing noises, while Stone and Dino kept a respectful distance. A moment later, the President of the United States swept into the room wearing a knockout black cocktail dress, quite low-cut, for a president.

"Now that you've all worshipped at the shrine of the latest member of the dynasty, can I force a drink on anyone?"

Everybody made affirmative sounds, and the butler supplied them with chilled liquids and comestibles.

"Well, now," Kate said, when she was settled on a sofa, "tell me how we can steal this beautiful necklace tonight."

58

Daryl Barnes stood in a line of male waiters and waited to be issued a uniform, while Annie waited in the female line. He stepped up to the issuer, who measured his chest and waist. "Forty and thirty-four," the man said. "Do you know your inseam? Save me the trouble?"

"Twenty-eight," Daryl replied.

The man went to a rack and extracted a red jacket and black trousers. The men had been told to arrive in a white shirt, black shoes, and black bow tie.

Daryl received the clothes and the key to a locker and went into the men's changing room. He dressed and found the uniform a good fit. He transferred the contents of his pockets to the uniform, including one item heavier than the others, regretting that he had been relieved of his switchblade at the metal detector. He wondered why a party would need a metal detector. He checked his glued-on mustache in the mirror, locked his locker, and went into the next room.

"Okay, you, you, you, and you will be serving dips," a woman said, including Daryl. "The rest of you will be taking orders for cocktails from those who don't want to stand in line at the bar, then delivering them. Please note that I am aware that all the booze tonight is premium stuff, and that may be tempting, but anybody trying to cop a bottle for later use will be ejected without pay. Everybody got that?"

Daryl had hoped for the dip. He collected a tray and was given a bowl of guacamole, then stocked his tray with chips. He could hear a pianist begin to play in the next room and the conversation of arriving guests. He walked into the room and began offering guests his tray, working his way toward the center of the space, where, like a beacon, the glitter of the Bloch-Bauer necklace drew him. He circled the little stand that held the post that bore the choker, under a glass lid, then continued to offer food until the bowl was nearly empty, when he returned to the kitchen for a new bowl.

Annie was on her way out with a tray of canapés, and he stopped for a moment. "All set? You know where the panel is?"

"Got it," she said, and went on her way.

As Daryl reentered the room the pianist stopped in the middle of a Cole Porter tune and began to play "Hail to the Chief." Ah, he thought, that explains the metal detector. He stopped in his tracks and watched the President of the United States enter the room, followed by her husband and a small group of people, one of whom was Stone Barrington. He resisted the urge to escape; his dyed hair and the mustache were disguise enough; Barrington would never recognize him.

Stone watched as Kate waved and nodded to the applauding crowd, then held up a hand to the pianist as if to say, "Enough." He went back to Cole Porter.

Stone then slowly steered Holly toward the necklace, glittering under the spotlight.

"My God!" Holly said. "I've never seen anything so . . . expensive. Wait a minute, I did see the Crown Jewels at the Tower of London once."

"The necklace would look good on you," Stone said. "We'll find out later."

Jamie Niven greeted the President and First Gentleman, then turned toward Stone. "Glad you could make it," he said, shaking hands.

"Jamie, this is Holly Barker, of the National Security Council. I've promised Holly and Vivian Bacchetti that, when this is over, they can try on the necklace. Can you arrange that?"

"Of course. My office is just down the hall — we can do that before it goes back into the vault."

Daryl continued his journey around the room. It occurred to him that, with the President in attendance, there would be Secret Service agents present, too, and he began to pick them out by the small discs in their lapels. They shouldn't be a problem, since their attention was focused entirely on the President. He served another bowl of guacamole and went back for a third refill. "Hey," he said to the supervisor, "since I can't steal any booze, can I have dibs on the leftover guacamole? My wife loves the stuff."

"Oh, sure, why not? The health department won't let us serve it again. There are some plastic containers over there."

Stone stood with Kate, Will, Dino, Viv, and Holly, looking at the necklace.

"That's what I want for Christmas," Kate said to Will.

"Well, let's see, if we sell the Georgetown house, the cattle farm, and the Carlyle apartment, that should get us within a few million of the price, but where would we live when you retire?" He steered her toward the smaller jewelry.

"This Carrie Fiske had quite an eye, didn't she?" Holly said, looking at a pair of diamond earrings.

"She did," Stone said, "but this is three generations of jewelry, so she didn't choose it all."

"I read the story about how the necklace got into her safe," Holly said. "Is it true?"

"As far as anybody can tell. Your agent's grandfather has been dead for a while, so all we have is Harvey's word for it."

"I understand you suspected poor Harvey of Carrie's murder."

"He was perfect for it — ex-husband cast aside, still in love with her, obsessive. Too bad you people alibied him out."

"He was in my old office in New York around the time of the murder," Holly said. "Did you want us to lie so you could put a good officer in prison for the rest of his life?"

"I think Dino would have found that convenient, but it wouldn't be his collar, anyway. A county sheriff in New Mexico will get that honor, if the guy can be caught."

"You have any doubts about that?"

"He's been on the loose his whole life and never been arrested. He's not going to make it easy for the police. I'm kind of hoping he'll try to steal it tonight, so I can grab him myself."

"Once a cop, always a cop," Holly said.

Now, carrying his tray, Daryl was working his way back toward the center of the room. He was only a few feet from the necklace when the lights went off.

59

Stone, who was wandering across the room when the lights went out, made for the necklace, but he was slowed twice by bumping into people in the dark. Later, he would figure that it took him half a minute to forty-five seconds to reach the display case. He was nearly there when the lights went on again. Jamie Niven had beaten him to the necklace by a second.

Jamie held up a hand, stopping Stone and two guards in dark suits. "It's all right," he said, pushing the guards back. "It was just a momentary power failure." A waiter offered him guacamole, but he waved it away.

"You're sure there's no problem?" Stone asked.

"Everything's fine, but I was glad to see that your reflexes were working."

"My heart hasn't slowed yet," Stone said, dabbing his forehead with a handkerchief. He rejoined his group.

"Your instincts were good," Dino said.

"How about yours? Where were you?"

"Relaxing," Dino said. "There are enough people in this room who would have handled it, if it had happened."

"I was hoping someone had stolen it," Will said. "That would have let me off the hook for Christmas."

Kate laughed. "Please don't think of yourself as off the hook, darling. The world has plenty of other baubles, and a lot of them are in this room." She looked at her watch: "We'll give it another few minutes, then decamp."

"If you'll forgive us," Stone said, "we're going to go to Jamie's office so that Holly and Viv can try on the necklace. Would you like to come?"

"Why torture myself further?" Kate said. "It's all right, dinner will wait for you."

Soon, Kate made her exit, and with that, others quickly followed. When the room had emptied of guests, Jamie removed the top of the display case, returned the necklace to its beautifully restored rosewood box, and beckoned for Stone's group to follow him. He led the way to his office, set the box on his desk, and turned. "Who's first?"

"I'm not shy," Viv said, stepping forward.

Jamie removed the necklace from the box

and unfastened the clasp; then he stopped. "Wait a minute," he said. "This is a new clasp, and I didn't approve that. The old one was working just fine." He turned his desk lamp toward him and looked more closely at the choker. "Oh, my God," he said.

Daryl and Annie helped clear the room of glasses and serving pieces, then Annie went to the ladies' dressing room. Daryl retrieved a plastic container from a pile and emptied the leftover guacamole into it from two serving dishes. He found a paper bag for the container, then went to the dressing room and retrieved his clothes, tossing his uniform into a laundry cart. He met Annie at the exit, where they were both given a cursory frisking for stolen liquor, then allowed to go to the service elevator.

"Everything okay?" Annie whispered.

"Couldn't be better," Daryl replied.

Jamie took a loupe from a desk drawer and trained it on the necklace. "It's a copy," he said, "and not a very good one."

"Good enough, apparently," Stone said.

"Who had access to the piece?" Dino asked, suddenly all cop.

"A number of people, but there was

always a security guard present, even when it was being cleaned."

Stone grabbed Dino's arm. "Come with me," he said, and sprinted from the office.

"Where are we going?" Dino asked.

They arrived in the display room, where the other pieces were being taken from their cases to be returned to the vault. Stone hesitated, then ran for the kitchen, bursting through the swinging doors. There was one man present, mopping the floor.

Stone turned and ran toward the foyer, then pressed a button for an elevator.

"Where are we going?" Dino asked again.

"To the service entrance," Stone replied. "It's a few doors down the street. Give me your backup piece."

"Are you kidding me?"

The elevator arrived and Stone dragged Dino into it. "All right, all right," Dino said. As the car started down, he knelt and yanked a Smith & Wesson Airweight .38 from its ankle holster and handed it to Stone.

"Is it loaded?" Stone asked, flipping open the cylinder.

"It's not a gun unless it's loaded," Dino said, taking a 9mm handgun from under his jacket.

The elevator door opened, and Stone ran

340

out, turning toward the service entrance, with Dino hot behind, clipping his badge to his tuxedo jacket pocket. They halted in front of the service entrance, looking up and down the street. Nobody.

"Who are we looking for?" Dino asked.

"A man — no, a man and a woman. Somebody had to turn off the lights."

"The lights were off no more than half a minute. You think somebody could lift the necklace and replace it in that time?"

"I wouldn't have thought so, but somebody did," Stone said.

The service door opened and a man and a woman stepped out; the man was carrying a paper bag.

"Let me do this," Dino said, "I'm legal, you're not." He stepped up to the couple, who stopped and looked at him uncomprehendingly. "Police," Dino said. "What's in the bag?"

"Guacamole," the man said. "I didn't steal it — the caterer said I could have the leftovers."

Stone took the bag from him and weighed it in his hand. "Pretty heavy guacamole," he said. He handed Dino the bag, then reached over and ripped the mustache from the man's face. "Look," he said to Dino, holding it up. "It's removable. Hi, Daryl."

Daryl drove a shoulder into Dino, knocking him back into Stone, staggering them both, then he ran like hell, with Annie right after him.

Stone pointed the Airweight at the base of a potted tree on the sidewalk. "Stop!" he yelled, then fired a shot into the tub's dirt.

"Next one goes into your back!" Dino yelled.

They came to a stop.

Dino's car pulled up next to them. "Anything I can do, Commissioner?" the driver asked.

"Arrest these two," Dino said. "Grand theft."

"*Very* grand theft," Stone echoed.

Back in Jamie Niven's office, Dino put the paper bag on the desk, removed a plastic container from it, and popped off the lid. He took a couple of tissues from a box on the desktop, spread them out, then picked up a letter opener and rummaged around in the guacamole. "If it's not here, this is going to be very embarrassing." He stopped, then scooped out the necklace and laid it on the tissues. It looked disgusting. "I believe this is yours," he said to Jamie.

"No," Jamie said, pointing at Stone, "it's his client's."

"My client would like it to have a bath," Stone replied.

60

On the appointed day, Stone sat at his desk and stared at his computer screen, which contained an image of the sale room at Sotheby's. Jamie Niven was at the lectern, and behind him, projected on a screen, was a detail of Klimt's *Woman in Gold* painting, showing a close-up of the necklace.

"And now," Jamie said, "we have the pièce de résistance of today's sale — the Bloch-Bauer necklace seen in the Klimt painting behind me."

The phone on Stone's desk buzzed, and Joan came on. "Sotheby's for you."

Stone pressed the speaker button. "Hello?"

The voice of a young woman. "Is this a customer ready to bid?"

"It is."

"May I have your customer number, please?"

Stone recited it to her.

"Are you ready to bid?"

"I am."

"Please confirm that your bidding will be capped at ten million dollars."

"Confirmed." Stone could see the young woman as she spoke at a table near Jamie Niven.

"This may be the most famous piece of jewelry in the world," Jamie was saying. "One of a kind, made by Bijoux Blume of Paris, in 1899. It is very nearly beyond price, but who will offer me five million dollars?"

The bidding began and quickly rose at first, in steps of a million dollars, then half a million.

"I have ten million five hundred thousand dollars," Jamie said.

Stone's heart sank.

"Who will bid eleven million?"

The young woman came back on the phone. "Bidder, do you wish to increase your bid?"

Stone gulped. "Eleven million dollars," he said.

"I have eleven million dollars," Jamie said. "Anything further?" He raised his gavel. "Last opportunity." He brought down the gavel. "Sold to a telephone bidder for eleven million dollars!"

The audience in the room burst into applause, and Stone fanned himself with a legal pad while he did some arithmetic. He buzzed Joan.

"Yes?"

"Call my broker and tell him to remove twelve million, six hundred and fifty thousand dollars from my money market account to my checking account."

"There's a fax from Sotheby's coming in now, asking for that amount and giving wiring instructions."

"Type up a letter to my bank instructing them to wire the funds, and fax it to them."

"Right."

Stone sat for a few minutes, still breathing hard. He looked at the invitation on his desk to a White House dinner.

Joan buzzed. "Your banker on the line."

Stone picked up the phone. "This is Stone Barrington."

"Mr. Barrington, I have received a fax on your letterhead instructing me to wire the sum of twelve million, six hundred and fifty thousand dollars to Sotheby's. Do you authorize this transaction?"

"I authorize it," Stone said.

"Thank you. The wire will go out within the hour."

Stone hung up, and Joan buzzed him immediately. "Jamie Niven on one."

Stone pressed the button. "Good morning, Jamie."

"Good morning, Stone, and congratulations! You've done very well for the Fiske estate."

"Thank you, Jamie, and my compliments on your conduct of the sale."

"Frankly, I thought it would go for nine million, maybe nine and a half."

"Fortunately, you had an idiot for a bidder. I've already instructed my bank to wire you the funds."

"We thank you for prompt payment. What disposition of the necklace would you like me to make?"

"You may messenger it to me at my office."

"It shall be done." The two men said goodbye and hung up.

Joan buzzed. "Holly Barker on one."

"Hello?"

"Good morning. I'm looking forward to seeing you tomorrow, and I've arranged the appointment you requested. The gentleman will be at the White House at five-thirty tomorrow. I'll meet you at the West Wing entrance and take you to him."

"Thank you."

"What is this all about, Stone?"

"You will know soon enough, but not too soon."

"Will your business take more than an hour? We're due in the family quarters at six, for drinks."

"I think not. We won't keep the Lees waiting."

"I'll see you then." They hung up.

Joan buzzed again. "A Sheriff Raimundo Martinez on line two."

Stone pressed the button. "Ray? How are you?"

"Very well, Stone. Last week I received a letter from the New York district attorney, offering my county first position for the prosecution of two people for the murder of Carrie Fiske."

"Congratulations."

"I've got ahold of a state airplane, and I'm going to complete the extradition in New York tomorrow. If you're around, I'll buy you a drink first."

"I'd like that, but I'm on my way to Washington, D.C., tomorrow for a dinner."

"In that case, all I have to do is to thank you for all your help in catching these people."

"You're very welcome, Ray, and if you're ever in New York again, I'll take you up on that drink." The two men said goodbye and hung up.

Joan appeared at the door. "I got a call from Sotheby's. There are two armed guards on the way over here with the necklace."

"That was fast," Stone said. "I guess they wanted to get rid of it as soon as possible."

61

Stone landed at Manassas, Virginia, at three PM, and what with traffic, arrived at the West Wing entrance to the White House a little before five, carrying his suitcase and a shopping bag. Holly came from her office to meet him, already dressed for dinner.

"The gentleman is waiting for you in the Situation Room," she said, kissing him. "It was the only room available. What's in the shopping bag?"

"You will see shortly."

She led him down the hall and into an ordinary-looking conference room.

"*This* is the Situation Room?" he asked. "I thought it would be underground and festooned with video monitors and flashing lights."

"Nope, this is it."

A well-dressed man was seated at one end of the table. He rose and offered his hand.

"Stone, this is Dr. Anthony Bill, the

350

secretary of the Smithsonian Institution. Dr. Bill, this is the President's friend, Stone Barrington."

The two men shook hands, and they all sat down. "I must say, Mr. Barrington," Dr. Bill said, "I'm a bit mystified as to the purpose of our meeting."

Stone set the shopping bag on the table, removed the rosewood box, and set it before Dr. Bill. "I wish to make an anonymous contribution to the Smithsonian," he said, then opened the box.

Bill gazed at the necklace for a moment. "My goodness," he said. "Of course, I recognize it. I watched the sale on closed-circuit television."

Stone took a legal-sized envelope from the shopping bag, opened it, and handed him a document. "This is a deed of gift, which states that only you may know the identity of the donor," Stone said. "It also provides that the necklace will reside at the White House, except at times when the Smithsonian wishes, with the permission of the President, to display it. It also specifies that the necklace is for the exclusive use of female presidents of the United States, first ladies and first daughters, and others, at the discretion of the President. If you find those terms acceptable, we can complete the transaction at this time."

Dr. Bill read the document quickly, took a pen from his pocket, and signed both copies. Stone signed them, gave one to Dr. Bill, then closed the box and returned it to the shopping bag. "Now, if you will excuse me, Dr. Bill, I will deliver this to the President."

"On behalf of the Smithsonian," Dr. Bill said, "I accept your incredibly generous gift, and I thank you most sincerely." They shook hands, Dr. Bill left, and Holly led Stone toward the family quarters.

"I guess this means that I'll never get to wear the necklace," she said.

"Perhaps the President will make an exception in your case."

"Did you really pay all that money for it, like the papers said?"

"Well, my fee as executor of Carrie Fiske's estate was a small percentage of its value, so it all evened out pretty well."

They took the elevator upstairs and were admitted to the family quarters by a Secret Service agent.

The Lees were seated in the living room, along with the British prime minister and his wife. Introductions were made and drinks ordered.

"Madam President," Stone said, reaching into the shopping bag. "I've brought you something to wear to the dinner tonight, if you choose to do so." He handed her the rosewood box.

Kate opened the box, and her jaw dropped. Stone handed her the deed of gift, and she read it and handed it to Will. She stood up and removed her necklace. "Stone, will you do the honors?"

Stone stood, placed the necklace around her neck, and secured it.

Kate looked in the mirror behind her. "A perfect fit," she said, then turned to her husband. "You, my darling, have a lot of catching up to do come Christmas."

AUTHOR'S NOTE

I am happy to hear from readers, but you should know that if you write to me in care of my publisher, three to six months will pass before I receive your letter, and when it finally arrives it will be one among many, and I will not be able to reply.

However, if you have access to the Internet, you may visit my website at www .stuartwoods.com, where there is a button for sending me e-mail. So far, I have been able to reply to all my e-mail, and I will continue to try to do so.

If you send me an e-mail and do not receive a reply, it is probably because you are among an alarming number of people who have entered their e-mail address incorrectly in their mail software. I have many of my replies returned as undeliverable.

Remember: e-mail, reply; snail mail, no reply.

When you e-mail, please do not send attachments, as I never open these. They can take twenty minutes to download, and they often contain viruses.

Please do not place me on your mailing lists for funny stories, prayers, political causes, charitable fund-raising, petitions, or sentimental claptrap. I get enough of that from people I already know. Generally speaking, when I get e-mail addressed to a large number of people, I immediately delete it without reading it.

Please do not send me your ideas for a book, as I have a policy of writing only what I myself invent. If you send me story ideas, I will immediately delete them without reading them. If you have a good idea for a book, write it yourself, but I will not be able to advise you on how to get it published. Buy a copy of *Writer's Market* at any bookstore; that will tell you how.

Anyone with a request concerning events or appearances may e-mail it to me or send it to: Publicity Department, Penguin Random House, 375 Hudson Street, New York, NY 10014.

Those ambitious folk who wish to buy film, dramatic, or television rights to my books should contact Matthew Snyder, Creative Artists Agency, 9830 Wilshire Boulevard, Beverly Hills, CA 98212-1825.

Those who wish to make offers for rights of a literary nature should contact Anne Sibbald, Janklow & Nesbit, 445 Park Avenue, New York, NY 10022. (Note: This is not an invitation for you to send her your manuscript or to solicit her to be your agent.)

If you want to know if I will be signing books in your city, please visit my website, www.stuartwoods.com, where the tour schedule will be published a month or so in advance. If you wish me to do a book signing in your locality, ask your favorite bookseller to contact his Penguin representative or the Penguin publicity department with the request.

If you find typographical or editorial errors in my book and feel an irresistible urge to tell someone, please write to Sara Minnich at Penguin's address above. Do not e-mail your discoveries to me, as I will already have learned about them from others.

A list of my published works appears on my website. All the novels are still in print in paperback and can be found at or ordered from any bookstore. If you wish to obtain hardcover copies of earlier novels or of the two nonfiction books, a good used-book store or one of the online bookstores can help you find them. Otherwise, you will have to go to a great many garage sales.

ABOUT THE AUTHOR

Stuart Woods is the author of more than sixty novels, including the *New York Times*–bestselling Stone Barrington and Holly Barker series. He is a native of Georgia and began his writing career in the advertising industry. *Chiefs*, his debut in 1981, won the Edgar Award. An avid sailor and pilot, Woods lives in New York City, Florida, and Maine.